RIVERSIDE DRIVE FOLLIES
and Other Stories

Eugene Lesser

skooBooks
los angeles

The author gratefully acknowledges Pamela Nittolo for both her creativity and plain hard work in bringing this book to fruition.

Photographs on front and back covers by Pamela Nittolo

Photograph of Golden Gate Bridge (AP Photo)
opposite page 179 by anonymous photographer

1st edition, 1st printing
9 8 7 6 5 4 3 2 1
ISBN: 978-0-9853400-2-5

For Lenny

Except for *Mel and Dee and the Great Unknown*, which appeared with a different title in Richard Hack's excellent literary magazine, Oxygen (Autumn, 1992), the novella and the other stories appear in print for the first time. Most of the novella was written in the 1962-1964 period. A half-century later I dusted it off and pruned it considerably but tried not to mess with it too much lest I lose the spark of what it was and who I was. *Mel Montrose: Live at the Carleton!* was also written in the 1990s but the other seven stories were written in the last few years.

The reader is advised to read the pieces in the order presented, mainly because all of them have the same protagonist, and the chronology reveals the evolution of character and events. Or maybe not, so read them any way you want.

Los Angeles
2018

Table of Contents

Prologue: What Did You Learn Today?

The final bell at Milford High School rang at 2:20. By 2:15 most of the kids had their backpacks ready, staring at the clock, ready to bolt. Mr. Wilkins, the 6th period history teacher, was always trying to squeeze in a tidbit more about the War of 1812 or the Reconstruction Act of 1867 but nobody was buying it. Mel Montrose was one of the few kids—the only kid-- who wasn't preparing to bolt. He didn't have a girlfriend, unless you count Nancy Rubin, a homework pal who wanted more than Mel could deliver. And most of the guys he knew either did have girlfriends or played ball and had practice right after school.

The 2:20 bell was too loud, Mel thought, and had a raspy sound, like a gargle. He sat in the front row and the kids from his aisle rushed past his desk. Buddy O'Hara, campus big shot, patted him on the back as he passed and said "Keep up the good work, Montrose." Mel knew he put something on his back but couldn't reach it. When Dickie Friedman passed he took off the post-it, stuck it on Mel's desk and kept walking. The post-it said, "I'm a faggot."

Mel walked the few blocks toward town where his father had a tailor shop—Quality Cleaners & Tailors. After his father had a couple of heart attacks, the doctors said he had to stop painting houses and hanging wallpaper so he re-invented himself as a tailor with a lot of help from Mel's sister. She had always made her own clothes and so she taught him how to put cuffs on pants and hem a dress and how to take in a waistline, using pins and a chip of soap to mark the spots. He opened a little shop and they set up sewing machines right next to each other. She could've gone to college but gave it up to work with him and keep an eye on him after his last heart attack. Mel felt he should at least help out in the store, waiting on customers and running errands, but he didn't always want to. In fact, he hardly ever wanted to, and he felt guilty about it.

Lately, though, he had different chores. His mother had what some of their friends and relatives called a nervous breakdown. Mel, his sister and their father never used that term. They didn't know what to call it. All her life she was fine, then one day she started acting strange. One time Mel was sitting on the couch and heard his parents talking in the kitchen about something. They weren't arguing or anything but she started saying things that didn't make any sense. After a while his father walked out of the kitchen, past Mel and up the stairs. He was crying.

The doctors recommended that she go for a while to the Fairfield State Hospital in Newtown, the place everyone called the "Funny Farm." We'd visit her on Sundays and sometimes on Wednesdays. But then we'd want her to come home. The thing is, she couldn't stay home alone and it was hard for her to stay in the shop. She'd say stuff to customers that sounded crazy. Inappropriate stuff like "I love you." So Mel's job was to meet her at the shop after school and take her home and be with her there. She could make her own food and stuff like that but they needed him to keep her company and talk with her and watch TV with her and play cards with her. She liked to play casino.

When Mel walked in the shop he gave his dad and sister a wave and walked over to his mother and gave her a big hug as always.

"Hi mom."

She took both of his hands and kissed them. Mel kind of liked that but sometimes she would do that with customers and they didn't know how to react.

Mel's father asked him, "What did you learn today?" That was a daily ritual. Usually Mel was stumped for an answer. Occasionally he'd offer something like, "I learned that James Buchanan was the only bachelor president." Or "I learned that Mrs. McGill assigns too much algebra homework." Today he said, "I didn't learn anything." And his father smiled, raised his eyebrows and said, "Then you should've stayed in bed." Without looking up from the sewing machine, Mel's sister said, "Don't give him any ideas."

After Mel gathered his backpack and his mother, they said their goodbyes and walked slowly over to the bus stop two blocks away. The family only had one car and Mel didn't have his driver's license yet so they always took the bus, which wasn't bad. They got dropped off right across from their house on Seaside Avenue.

The bus stop was right in front of the Milford library,

and all the kids who lived in Fort Trumbull or Walnut Beach or Devon would gather there on the benches and on the library steps. This was the hard part for Mel. He got nervous about any encounters with the kids from school. He always hoped the bus would come quickly and they could sit in front where the kids usually didn't sit and get home without any interactions. But sometimes one of his classmates would walk up to him and ask him about the homework assignment or something like that. Mel would try to answer them as quickly as possible, hoping they would just leave, but some lingered and inevitably would say hello to Mel's mother, and she would inevitably say something that just made no sense at all and Mel would laugh nervously and change the subject.

He always worried that, by now, after taking his mother home on a bus so many times, the kids who had even brief contact with her would start talking about her. Stuff like, "Have you met Mel Montrose's mother? She's weird."

On this particular day the bus was unusually late. As more and more kids gathered, Mel got more and more nervous. Walking out of the library with his cheerleader girlfriend on his arm was none other than Buddy O'Hara. Mel quickly turned away, suddenly interested in the cloudy sky. But instead of walking by, Buddy stopped and, with a pronounced smirk, said,

"Hey, Mel, is this your mother?"

"Yes."

"Nice to meet you, Mrs. Montrose," and held out his hand.

Mel's mother took his hand, brought it up to her mouth and kissed it three times with great feeling before Buddy pulled it away, overwhelmed and frightened. She looked up at him and said, "I love you." He laughed nervously and turned away, pulling his girlfriend with him.

The bus finally came. Mel found a double seat up front as usual and put his arm around his mother protectively. They both stared out the window as the bus drove along the long village green. His mother broke the silence.

"Your friend is such a nice boy."

After a pause: "Yeah. He really is, mom."

Now he put both arms around her as the bus turned down Seaside Avenue, his head resting on her shoulder.

Our Decade

After my father died in 1958, three years after my mother, I was all messed up. I was 21 and supposed to be a man. At first I left school, left my job at the East Side Bus Terminal, left my apartment and spent some time back in Milford, helping out my sister who ran Quality Cleaners and Tailors by herself now. For a minute it felt good to see some of my old buddies, but I was like Ishmael in *Moby Dick*. Whenever I got the urge to methodically knock people's hats off, then I had to get, not to the sea, but back to Manhattan.

So I got back. At first I worked at a movie theater-- the Jefferson on 14th near Third Avenue--where they mostly had me counting people coming into the theater. One movie was *The Ten Commandments* and there were three or four daily screenings. I had a little counter in my hand which I furtively held in my pocket. Click click click. Oooh clandestine. After the show started I recorded the numbers in a ledger. That led to working as an assistant manager at the Riviera theater uptown at 97th and Broadway. For lunch I'd stroll over to the nearby Senator Cafeteria and have a ham salad sandwich. 35 cents, I think it was. I was living pretty close by—88th between Columbus and Amsterdam. I could walk to work.

Later, near the end of 1959, I moved to a studio apartment on West 75th Street, near West End Avenue. I had a new job as a psychiatric nurse's aide working the midnight–to-eight shift at the Payne

Whitney Psychiatric Clinic. The clinic, part of what was then known as the New York Hospital, was on the opposite side of Manhattan--in the East 60s near the river. A lot of celebrities checked into the Payne Whitney. Marilyn Monroe and Marlon Brando, to name two, spent time there. Also Robert Lowell, Mary McCarthy, lots of well-known people.

The patients were sleeping during much of my shift, but there were always stragglers, sleepwalkers and special problems. And they got up early, most of them by six o'clock. I used to monitor the guys in the bathrooms and showers and when they were shaving. One morning I was absent-mindedly whistling a song when the great Rube Bloom threw his razor down and marched over to me and told me to stop whistling that song. Sure, Rube, whatever you say. I was whistling a Harry Warren tune, *There Will Never Be Another You*. Warren and Rube were contemporaries and New Yorkers, and probably knew each other, so maybe Rube didn't like him or was jealous. He had no reason to be. Bloom wrote some of my favorite songs—*Fools Rush In, Day In--Day Out, Don't Worry 'Bout Me, Give Me the Simple Life*. He was also a good piano player and singer in his day. He had his own band and played with different guys. Bix Beiderbecke, for one. I wanted to hug the guy but he wasn't approachable like that.

The girlfriend, maybe wife, can't remember, of bop trumpeter Blue Mitchell also worked the graveyard shift. We had some great chats. At two, three, four in the morning on the floor with nothing much going on, it's easy to talk, and listen. I also got friendly with some nurses. notably Betty Semansky. She dug lying together on my bed (on *top* of the blankets) and getting really hot. Not as a prelude to sex but as an end in itself. Sex, as we usually think of it, was out of bounds. Kind of a theme with me—Catholic girls who are horny but don't do sex. Occasionally I got to first base, sometimes even got to second base but whenever I tried to stretch a double into a triple I got thrown out by twenty feet. Dry humping was about the pinnacle, the Everest.

At a New Year's Eve party ushering in 1960, I met Ben Rosen and Allison O'Connor, a couple that lived on 71st Street, only a few blocks from me. We immediately hit it off and started seeing each other a lot. Ben was finishing up his doctorate in art history at Columbia, and Allison was a red-diaper baby from a family of union organizers and hell-raisers. She was carrying the torch as an office manager of a progressive law firm in midtown. Allison, salt of the earth, was really good-looking but you had to notice it. She played it way down, no doubt understanding that that had the greatest effect. She wore sensible shoes, even sensible high heels. Her skirts ended way below the knee. She wore no makeup and pulled her hair straight back in a bun. Allison looked right at you. She was honest and no-nonsense but with a warm vibe. I really dug her.

Sometimes on weekend mornings I'd go over to their place and have breakfast with them. One time I was over there after spending the entire night with Betty Semansky playing let's-see-how-hot-we-can-get-without-actually-having-sex. Allison made coffee and I started telling them about my week and got around to the previous night's non-sex. Allison's response, serious and sympathetic, was "Mel, you probably need to masturbate. Feel free to use our bathroom." I wasn't as open and honest as she was so I didn't take her up on it.

Ben was influenced by Allison but he also had a strong working-class background. He had gone to non-prestigious City College and dressed in a kind of proletarian uniform: blue denim work shirt, black tie, black jacket. He was close to getting his Ph.D. He only had to finish his thesis and pass his foreign language requirement. He had already won a Fulbright scholarship that was to start in September in Frankfurt. He chose to study in Germany because he was scared shitless of Germany and all things German. Scared but obsessed. If you're Jewish you probably know the drill. And World War II was still in the air. It had ended only 15 years earlier. He felt he had to go there, confront it, finally deal with it.

I learned a lot from Ben, especially art history. We went to museums and cruised the galleries on 57th Street and the east side. I remember going to a gallery that showed Franz Kline's new stuff. He was famous for his paintings that featured a few (sometimes just two or three) wide brush strokes of black paint, with drips, on a white canvas. On this day we saw Kline's brand new thing: the introduction of...*color*. In this case, green. Some bold gashes of Kelly green were added to the black and white milieu. Very exciting. Ben also turned me on to one of his professors, Mischa Ernst. I started sitting in on Ernst's classes. I just showed up at the big lecture hall and sat in back.

I remember Ben and me hitch-hiking out of Manhattan in a full-on blizzard on our way to a museum in Philadelphia that had a big Thomas Eakins retrospective. The storm was so bad we figured that by the time we arrived the museum might close down. But we were up for about anything back then. Early on he asked me to come with him to Europe. He wanted to see Paris and other places a bit before starting his Fulbright year in September. "Let's go in June and spend the summer running around. We'll be the two musketeers." So that was the plan.

Ben and Allison threw little parties—the vibe was more like a salon--where the conversations were about the art world, radical politics, foreign movies (Bergman, Kurosawa, Fellini) and lefty periodicals (Partisan Review, Dissent, I.F. Stone's Weekly, Monthly Review). If anyone mentioned an article from one of those mags, the rest of them had already read it. Bruno Petroff, later a professor at the University of Chicago and a prominent art critic, was a regular, as was Jake Horwitz, another guy who later became prominent, at Penn State I think. I grew up on literature, which surprisingly they weren't into, except political stuff like Orwell or Camus. I was also into jazz while they went more for classical. So their shtick was new to me and I ate it up.

At one of these get-togethers I met Chloe, a close

friend of Allison's. Chloe, like Allison, was a couple of years older than I was and it showed. She spoke French and dug the French composers—Debussy, Ravel, and she played her record of Saint-Saens' violin concerto for me—but she also dug jazz. Another thing she dug was sex. The night we met I saw her home on a subway back to the Bronx. She invited me up for a glass of wine and got right to work, immediately assuming the role of sexual mentor, which impressed me because she must've picked up that I needed one. She took her time and so did I. I waited for her cues. We were going at it pretty good when she said, and it was the first time I had ever heard the expression, "Shall I assume the position?" That was hot. I started pounding away but she slowed me way down and that was even better. I kept at it nice and slow and I could see she was feeling it. And then she said, "You can plow me now."

So I plowed her.

Chloe was into lots of guys but we got together several times over the next few months. We went to Birdland a couple of times, and she knew some people on the east side who threw parties that she took me to, wanting to show me what life was like on the other side of the park. Yeah, people with for-real paintings by Braque and Matisse on the walls. Sometimes with a live trio in one of the rooms. Hip shit. Chloe got my mind off Betty Semansky.

One day Ben asked me to meet him at a bar on Broadway near 72nd. He had met this fellow doctoral candidate, Sally, that he had the hots for. She had gone to Vassar and came from money, the anti-Allison. He had actually mentioned her to Allison in a casual context. I know because I was there. But it didn't stand out. He always talked to Allison about school, his professors, his fellow students, some funny thing that someone said. But a couple of nights later he mentioned her again and I know Allison picked up on it that time. He started seeing Sally after classes and occasionally in the evening on some pretext. In the bar I asked him why he mentioned her a second time and actually a third time. He said he just couldn't help himself. Kind of like a criminal who wants to get caught. That made me see how gone on her he was. He was torn between keeping the affair a secret and wanting to tell the world that he was banging the most desirable chick in Manhattan. The outline of it reminded me of *A Place in the Sun* in which Montgomery Clift, a working-class lug, whose girlfriend is the kvetchy, plain-looking and pregnant Shelley Winters, meets the glittery rich and beautiful Elizabeth Taylor. All downhill from there. It bothered me to think Ben was cheating on Allison, who worked hard and even supported him. But I could see he couldn't help himself, so crazy was he for this Sally. Finally I met her and very quickly understood the situation. Sally was gorgeous and brilliant. Let's pause right there. She was also funny *and* witty, and seemed like a nice person on top of that. Yeah, Ben had a major problem.

Over the next few months, Ben was in masquerade mode. He tried to be kind and attentive to Allison but was jonesing on Sally full-time. He told Sally of his plans to go to Europe with me and asked her to join us—the third musketeer. She said it sounded good but she had some commitments in early June that she might not be able to get out of. In the weeks before we sailed, Ben hadn't heard much from her, so we assumed she wouldn't be joining us. I thought one reason might be because I would be a third wheel and not that much fun for her.

I was standing in Ben and Allison's apartment, straddling my suitcase, watching them hugging and saying how much they were going to miss each other. A nice warm scene but I knew that if Sally was on that ship Ben and Allison were done and that was their last hug.

We made our way down to the pier, went on board and found our room. After throwing our suitcases on our beds we walked up to the main deck. It was a beautiful afternoon. We were admiring the view when Sally popped up with a wild cathartic grin, a bottle of champagne in one hand and three champagne glasses in the other hand. She had stolen both handfuls from the main dining room. The handful of three glasses touched me. It established us as a trio.

The ship started moving out of the harbor and we took in the southern tip of Manhattan and the surrounding panorama. I'd taken the ferry to Staten Island and certainly enjoyed the view but to be on this ship leaving the harbor, leaving the panorama, leaving

New York...we all got a lump in our throat as we drifted farther and farther away from shore. We filled our glasses and Sally delivered the toast. "This is our decade," she announced. We lifted our glasses and she said, "To *us*," and Ben and I repeated it, like an oath.

And so our voyage started and so the Sixties began for us. For the next two-and-a-half months we gamboled through Europe with great camaraderie a la *Jules and Jim*. We all dug each other but it was just Ben and Sally doing the sex thing. I was their sidekick. Gabby Hayes.

From Le Havre we took a train into Paris and wound up staying at a little hotel right on Pont Neuf. I was impressed when Sally started talking rapid-fire French to the concierge.

We started hitting the museums every day. You'd be an oaf if you couldn't learn from Ben and Sally. Even when they disagreed, which was often, it was fascinating to hear their arguments and *how* they argued. They were both very sure of themselves. They would have loads of fun chuckling over a painting they thought was a fake, or a painting that said "attributed to," say, Giotto. They'd say, "not even close," and move on. Case closed. We're done here.

We went to the Louvre a lot and the Impressionist museum, then called the Jeu de Paume. We walked through the Rodin Museum with its sculptures inside and outside, beautifully integrated in its gardens. We strolled through Gustave Moreau's atelier. More than once in our museum-hopping Ben and Sally bumped into a colleague or two from Columbia, which was uncomfortable because all of them knew Allison. All except Sally.

One of our favorite activities was to steal books at Brentano's, a big English-language bookstore near the embassy. Sally was fearless. I'd get a couple of paperback books in my backpack and call it a day's work but Sally always walked in with one of those huge department store shopping bags and loaded it up with books, her jacket draped over the bag. She had that patrician look that no one dared question. On the bedside table in our hotel rooms were the books we stole from Brentano's. And we read them, too. We all dug going off and reading, usually in the long afternoons. Later we'd report on what we read.

The weather was very hot in Paris, so we decided to go to Spain, first to Barcelona, and figure it out from there. The night before we left we went out to a few bars, then wound up back at the hotel, my room, with two or three bottles of wine, and got smashed. Somehow we decided to dress up with whatever was around in some character and become that person. Sally went into prostitute mode, wearing a beret, a lavender blouse with a deep décolleté, exaggerated makeup and looked, well, beautiful. Ben tied a yellow bandana around his head and did a Cuban revolutionary thing, and also looked pretty authentic. I wore some kind of hat, I forget, but my persona was jazz singer. I did a Joe Williams version of *Roll 'em, Pete.* (*I got a girl who lives up on a hill*...) from a record I had called Joe Williams Sings, Count Basie Swings.

They both were kinda shocked that I sounded so good. Ben said he was going to introduce me to a guy who runs a jazz club in the Village. Though I sang a lot growing up with my buddies, this was the first time I thought of myself as a "singer." That game we played changed me, and I think taking on those personas changed Ben and Sally too, though we never talked about it. Funny, we talked about everything. Both of them had been in analysis. Talking about stuff was what you did in those days. But that game we played ran deep, deeper than we realized.

We caught a train to Barcelona and really enjoyed that city. We strolled the Ramblas, went to jazz clubs, Guell Park, Sagrada Familia, but it was pretty hot in Spain too, so Sally had the bright idea of going on a 14-hour boat ride to Menorca in the Mediterranean, one of the Balearic Islands, the better known of which were Ibiza and Mallorca.

When we arrived on Menorca we went straight over to our two-story Bauhaus-style chalet right on the water that we rented back on the mainland from an architect who designed the building. After impressing me with her fluency in French, Sally showed equal prowess with her elegant Spanish as she handled the tricky rental negotiations.

In the morning I'd wake up to waves lapping on the shore near my window. When we walked over to the *mercado* and introduced ourselves, the storekeeper, who was born there, told us that, though he had seen English-speaking people, British and Australians, we were the first Americans he could remember, and that was Mahon, the port and main town. Yeah, everyone went to Ibiza or Mallorca. Nowadays more and more American tourists go to Menorca. I like to think we discovered the place.

Each day, usually late afternoon, we'd walk into town and check out the plaza scene. There was often some kind of festival. One time we were sitting in folding chairs set up like a peanut gallery when I first saw bats. They'd flit down under the seats. While we freaked out, bolting from our chairs, Ben covering his neck so as not to be bitten by vampire bats, no one else paid the slightest attention to the bats.

We brought a lot of those Brentano's books with us and read on the beach, in our cool bedrooms, and on our patio. When our monthly rental ended we returned to Paris and spent another couple of weeks there until September, the beginning of Ben's Fulbright year.

Before Ben went to Frankfurt he had a one-week orientation in Berlin. He wanted me to go with him. I had planned on flying out of Paris when Ben left for Germany, and I was running low on money, but Ben figured I could crash in his hotel room in Berlin. That would be the biggest expense. So I did. I had to see Berlin, stand on the Kurfurstendamm and let it all sink in. I had that revulsion-attraction to Germany that Ben had, just a milder form.

Sally had a return ticket to fly back home, so we said our goodbyes in Paris. She gave me a peck on the

17

cheek and told me what fun she had. She and Ben hugged each other, a passionate hug that reminded me of Allison and Ben hugging before we left. Sally was hardly out the door before her absence was felt. The triangularity of us created a thriving social unit, a genre, which turned the inherent awkwardness of two-lovers-and-a-sidekick into something pretty cool. In fact, we were one hell of a trio.

At that time, the US did not have diplomatic relations with East Germany so the embassy wouldn't give us travel visas. In fact, they discouraged us from going to East Germany at all but especially on a train. See, there was West Germany and East Germany, and Berlin, though part of the west, was like an island in the middle of the east zone. Thus, on a train you'd have to cross "enemy" territory. The guy at the embassy looked gravely at me and said, "Anything can happen in there and if you get in trouble, we can't help you." I loved that "in there." Like East Germany was some kind of horrible pit. We knew that everything he said was bullshit. Anyway, flying was too expensive.

Trains were expensive, too, so we thought we could save some money if we hitch-hiked out of France, through Belgium to the West German border (maybe Cologne and see the cathedral), then take trains from there. The next morning we got on a bus that took us to a highway on the far northeast side of Paris. We knew it might take a while to get a ride so we got up early, had our suitcases ready, and the bus dropped us off on the highway before ten o'clock.

There we were in the utter boonies of Paris, and boy were we not getting any rides. After five or six hours we started reviewing Plans B and C. When it looked like we were losing daylight we had to accept the harsh truth. Carrying our suitcases (they didn't have wheels then) we walked back to where the bus dropped us off and rode back into Paris and went right over to the Gare du Nord and bought tickets on an overnight train to Berlin. Leaving in an hour.

At the East German border, the moment we were waiting for, the train came to a stop. A guy with a red star on his hat climbed on board with one of those change dispensers that the Good Humor man wore around his waist, or people at carnival booths. He was walking down the aisle saying, "...visas...visas..." He stopped at our seat and said in English, "Good evening. Welcome to East Germany." He knew we were Americans. Everyone instantly recognizes Americans. The way we dress, the way we move. I didn't dig that. I wanted more anonymity. But that's how it goes when you're so dramatically *overt*. We bought visas for three or four bucks and that was that. So much for grave warnings by embassy hacks.

Pulling into Berlin on a train at night was full of drama. Fucking wow. This was the heart of the evil. Somehow I could feel it. Seeping through the concrete.

It didn't take long before Ben had his first traumatic experience. Welcome to Germany. As we walked through the grand lobby of the train station, the loudspeaker came on to announce trains departing and arriving but it was in German, natch, and the sound of German can seem harsh. Portuguese it ain't. The announcements began with a loud and strident "Achtung! Achtung!..." Ben lost it right there. For the first time I realized how serious this problem was, not only for Ben but for me, too. Hearing those words evoked Auschwitz, Anne Frank, man's inhumanity to man.

In a couple of days we showed up at the hotel where Ben and all the other Fulbright scholars in Germany were to stay and get their orientation. Security was lax at the hotel. There was no list and I never had to show ID. It was assumed that I was also a Fulbright scholar. And I developed a spiel that I gave to anyone who asked during, say, dinner: I'm studying the early years of Albrecht Durer. Ben could always bail me out if I got in over my head. I slept on a couch in Ben's room and ate for free in the dining room with all the others.

A big kick was walking over to East Berlin right through the Brandenburg Gate. We were among the last tourists to go freely from west to east, or east to west. The following April, the Berlin Wall was built and it stayed up for nearly 30 years. We used to go over to the Humboldt University area and hit the cafes where students hung out. We would engage those who spoke English. Most of them did. While West Berlin was all cleaned up, sparkling, a phoenix-like showcase of the West that revealed few signs of the war's devastation, East Berlin kept its side gritty. The commies left rubble on empty lots and even on some streets. They wanted to remind everyone of what war is. The east's economy was dramatically worse than the west's. I remember talking with a young woman, a student, who said, "The west has a better life but we have a better idea."

We also went to the opera in East Berlin and, for a couple of bucks, saw Mozart's *Cosi Fan Tutti*. I dug the tiny and elegant opera house. It was a surprise to see something so magnificently done in such an intimate setting.

The time finally came when Ben and I said our goodbyes. He took a train to Frankfurt and I took a train to the U.S. embassy in Hamburg. I told them I was broke and needed a way back. They offered to loan me the money, $120, I think it was, and I would pay them back—in installments. They placed me on a ship that was taking discharged soldiers back home via the Brooklyn Navy Yard. From Hamburg I took a train to Bremerhaven where the ship docked. I had to wait a few days before it left so I stayed at this city-run soup kitchen that was underground, built originally as a bomb shelter during the war. I played chess most of the time with two or three old-timers who were happy to see new blood.

Once on the ship I slept with the soldiers in bunks that went up four-high but the rest of the time I could go to the other side of the ship where officers and some civilians hung out in relative luxury. When the guys stepped off that boat they were civilians and they couldn't wait, but until then they were still soldiers.

This lame sergeant took pleasure in harassing them for the slightest thing right to the end. They all hated him. One morning he jabbed me in the ribs telling me to get my ass up. I screamed at him. "I am a civilian. Keep your fucking hands off me." He backed off and those guys loved me after that.

As the coast came into view and New York harbor loomed, I re-ran everything the three of us did over the last three months. What joy. But I was oblivious of what was to come:

After Ben returned the following June I went to see him up in the Bronx where he was staying with his parents. Aside from noticing that he was acting strange, my first clue that something was up was when he mentioned that he'd been back for a couple of weeks. I figured he'd get in touch right away. I had called Allison, who also hadn't heard from him but heard he was back. If so, I figured he'd be staying with his parents, so I called. He had already gotten a couple of great job offers, like curator of modern art at a big-time museum.

We walked across the street to a neighborhood park and sat on a bench. His unfriendliness shocked me. And everything I said he deemed wrong or dumb. I told him I was getting interested in nature, learning the names of trees. He immediately pointed to the nearest tree and said, "What kind of tree is that?" I looked but couldn't identify it. When I said I didn't know he kind of sneered. Then he pointed to another tree. I didn't know that one either. I saw his face grimace as if to say, you're just a bullshitter who doesn't know a damn thing. That's when it all became clear to me. Ben was cutting me loose, along with his blue denim work shirts. He was about to enter the glittery world of administrators, trustees, critics, media, donors, money, and lots of women like Sally. And here I was, a dropout with no career goals, a fucking boho who could only drag him down. He was officially cutting all ties with me. Then I remembered I also had that same feeling when we said our goodbyes in Berlin. He was going to Frankfurt to launch his career and I was returning to New York--to do what exactly? I guess there is no cool way to tell a guy you no longer want to be friends.

Strange to say, I never saw Ben again. Nor did I ever see Sally again, who dumped me for the same reason though she may not have even noticed, so different were our worlds. Nor did Ben re-connect with Sally. The three of us were so close, then suddenly out of each other's lives forever.

As the big ship maneuvered into its berth at the Brooklyn Navy Yard I reviewed my resources. Three dollars and change. I figured I'd take a subway up to the Columbia area and look for my buddy Alex. See what he's up to.

Riverside Drive Follies

A Novella

If you care too much about what you have to say, if your heart is too much in it, you can be pretty sure of making a mess. You get pathetic, you wax sentimental...feeling, warm heartfelt feeling, is always banal and futile; only the irritations and icy ecstasies of the artist's corrupted nervous system are artistic.

--Thomas Mann, *Tonio Kroger*

Manhattan

Friday, December 16, 1960

Chapter One

"Ohhhhhhhhhhhhhhhhhhhhhhhhh
Cream O' Wheat is so good to eat.
Yes we have it every day.
We sing this song as we walk along
and it makes us shout 'hooray.'
It's good for growing babies
and grownups, too, to eat.
For all the family's breakfasts,
you can't beat Cream O' Wheat."

He drags out the tempo on the last line. Just to bug me.

"Good morning, Let's Pretenders...God, what a sewer...Mel?..."

Untimely ripp'd from my nighty-night.

"Cream O' Wheat, it turns out, is now Cream *of* Wheat. That's the kind of world it is, and you can't make it go away by feigning sleep...ech, your hosiery is a slap in the face...Mel?...Mel..."

I breathe slowly, deeply, even my mouth is slightly open. Boy, am I feigning.

"I have news that may change the very tenor of our lives."

Say, Akira, are you sure this Yank is dead?...Search me, Hideo, why don't you turn him over like a steak with the bayonet on your rifle and find out...Oh, all right... Watch out you don't ironically pierce the photograph of his best girl. He turns me over like a steak, ironically piercing the photograph of my best girl.

"There's a telegram for you from an Alvin Dark...Seriously, I've got a major announcement... Mel?..."

If Richie hadn't woken me up I would've forgotten my dream like I usually do. The headline said "Montrose Pleads Guilty." A mob was chasing me through Grand Central Station. I ran into the men's room and saw my father washing his hands at a sink. He looked up and saw me in the mirror and then looked back down. He didn't recognize me. I needed to take a dump but there were only pay toilets and I didn't have a dime. I tried climbing over the stall, lost my balance and fell into the toilet, head first, straight down the pipes into hell or wherever people like me end up.

"Your room represents a new *zenith* in squalor."

He's making his A move now, zeroing in. He knows I get nervous when his cloven hooves are near my glasses on the floor. I can hear him breathe.

"Amazing. Moss is actually growing around your mouth."

It'll be a while before the blood bank will do business with me again, so any injury to my glasses would be a fiscal disaster. My optometrists should hang by their scrota until motionless. Clyne & Rosetree: Stylists In Eyewear. Humiliating, trying to pass. Why bother? The gentiles can spot you a mile away. Eyewear fashions for fall.

"Mel?...*Mel!*...This room is a piece of *work*. I guess you have to hate yourself to live like this...your undergarments, my god...Mel, you know I wouldn't arbitrarily disturb your sleep, and maybe you were right last night, about me crying wolf but everybody's crying wolf. That's not what I have to say right now but I just happened to think of it, and you're crying wolf by testing me to see how I'll react to your puerile attempts at--"

"Get the fuck out."

"Ah, Mel."

Provoked into utterance. Unforgivably careless.

"Even in anger, the sound of your voice is reassuring...Let me tell you what happened."

Phlegm has one scared little vowel, trying to hang around with the big guys. I open an already balled up Kleenex from the floor and spit my morning lunger into it. There's no stopping him now.

"A sweeping development has taken place."

I rub my middle finger in my belly-button and sniff it. Why does my belly-button smell like a vagina?

"You're going to flip when I tell you."

The glasses each morning. Cold frames in the winter. To think we see all there is to see through two little eyes, a couple of knotholes in the fence. Back-to-school eyewear.

"G'mornin', Mel," he says with mock warmth.

"Waiter, there's a black rectilinear rodent in my soup."

"It's an old Basque recipe."

If there was anything worse than being a fuckin' Hebe it was being a fuckin' *four-eyed* Hebe. Myopia ruined my life and who cares? In that era glasses were considered uncool. "Hey, four eyes!" When I played basketball they made me wear these grotesque goggles. Antihero I think was the brand name. Then one pasty winter day you realize you don't play ball anymore. Or if you do your shoes slide on the asphalt and you don't care. It doesn't count anymore. And the ball belongs to this kid with white sneaks who thinks you must have been pretty good. Better than you were.

"Wait'll I tell ya."

"What do I smell?"

"My casserole. Au vin. Just a pinch."

"What is it, six o'clock or something?

"It's way past 7:30."

"Who do I hear in the kitchen?"

"Alex, working on his matrix. Poor devil."

Someday I'll tell the whole story. The Cleveland Plain Dealer will call it a hip *David Copperfield.* I'll be taught in a class called The Naturalist Agony, MWF 2:00—3:00 (text: *Shitty Underwear and the Urban*

Ethos: Selections from Dreiser, Zola, Sinclair, Montrose et al).

"I want to tell you what happened."

"The money's coming in Monday?"

"You're caustic this morning."

"Spit it out."

"Dig this," he says with a shit-eating grin. "I went over to see a certain well-known personage last night."

"Since I'm not interested in the first place, I'm not likely to be in suspense."

"The touched-up gray eminence of Laura Longstreet."

"She's retired. She already went through that."

"I keep forgetting how naive you are in these matters."

"Is she interested or what?"

"Does a hobby horse have a wooden asshole?"

"Yes, but is she interested?"

"Not only *interested*, but—direct quote—*excited about the project*."

"I want to brush my teeth."

"She *loved* the script."

"She said that?"

"In so many words."

"She rang for the doorman."

"How wrong you are."

"She thought you were fatuous."

"She said the script was *viable*."

"Tell me if she's going to do the part or not and let me brush my teeth."

"You've got to know the context."

"Believe me, I don't want to know the context."

"Let me tell you. It's a kick in the head."

"I don't want to hear it."

"*Please.*"

"Oh, don't beg."

"*Please.*"

"All right, give me the fucking context."

"Good."

"Brevity."

"Right. I grab a cab to her redoubt at Beekman Place. I'm a very carefully planned one hour late because if I weren't how then could I have been unable to break away from an investor or been tied up at CBS helping them cut a documentary? I feel imperially slim walking across the lobby as the elevator man touches his visor obsequiously."

"This is nuts."

"I'm handsome semen shooting up the urethra of the Beekman Tower as I soar to the 18th floor."

"Paraguay has six navigable rivers."

"A tasteful push on the buzzer and I'm Cary Grant, whistling a tune--*Getting To Know You*, actually, from *The King And I*--"

"Gee, aren't you going to say 'by Rodgers and Hammerstein'?"

"--unexplainably interested in my hatband."

"That's *it*."

"You've got to picture her opening the door and standing there in her brocaded Cassini lounging togs with a--"

"*Stop* it."

"*Please*."

"One sentence!"

"Laura promised me positively that she will sign a contract when the money comes in."

I've been "in care of" Richie Kovak--that's how I get my mail---since September. On that day I got off the boat from Europe with less than five bucks in my pocket. I took a subway to the upper west side around Columbia where I transferred after two years at UConn. When my father died I dropped out of school and most everything else. I was nursing a beer at the West End when Richie passed by and recognized me at the bar. We had met once through Alex, who I was looking for. Turned out Alex was staying at Richie's 454 Riverside Drive pad. There was a tiny living space on the other side of the kitchen that Richie offered to me rent-free until I got back on my feet. It was providential, he told me, that our paths should cross again at precisely that point in his career because the following Monday he was going to get the $195,000 he needed to make his movie.

"You don't look pleased."

"You woke me up for this?"

"I was hoping you'd share in enjoying the good news."

"But you haven't got the bread and you're not even close to getting it."

"The wheels are *turning*."

Motherfucker is certifiable.

"Occasionally," he yells, first at me, then out the door, his voice booming through the whole flat, "Occasionally I do need a word of encouragement. I admit that character flaw. Consider, then, the gross irony to be surrounded by jackals and philistines."

He turns back to me.

"Look at yourself. You're *effete*."

Alex, from the kitchen, says in a devastatingly calm voice that he's trying to read. Richie runs out screaming at him, calling him a parasite and a Quisling. Then, down the hall, he goes into the living room and starts yelling at Norman.

I think of the brutal wind that must be whipping around the corner of 116th. My father died after his third heart attack, aggravated by severe asthma. Smoking Pall Malls down to the ash didn't help. He was buried next to my mother who died of ALS three years earlier when I was 18. After my father died I couldn't face anything. I wanted to throw in my hand and get five new cards. A few days after the funeral a buddy of mine drove me down to Wilmington, North Carolina where I caught a slow freighter to Liverpool. A hundred and twelve bucks. Sixteen days at sea. I looked deep into my soul but I couldn't see anything.

I hit London and went straight to Piccadilly to shake the monkey off my back and get laid. I lost my cherry with a buxom blond who wouldn't even take off her bustier, or whatever you call it. She said, "You can still get to the pussy." Later she told me that she would have taken it off if she had known I was a virgin. London was great and so was Madrid, mostly because I didn't know anyone for 3000 miles. Sometimes I could forget that I was me. In Madrid I met this cat from San Francisco, Don Gamble, who was studying Spanish at the Instituto. We would hit the bars together and got pretty close. He told me if I ever made the move out to Frisco I could stay with him. That sounded good.

Richie returns. He really needs to lose weight.

"You look like a chess piece," I tell him.

"Oh?"

"A rook."

"But I move only on the diagonals."

"You gotta start doing the push-aways."

"After you brush your teeth I'll tell you about last night."

Richie, as usual, has been up all night. He not only never sleeps, he doesn't like anyone *thinking* he does. Once, mid-afternoon, while he took one of his rare and brief naps, the phone rang and I answered and this--as I was later to find out—gorgeous female asked for Richie and I told her he was napping. She hung up, and three minutes later Richie was up wondering if the phone rang. I told him that the--as it turned out—gorgeous female called and the horrible thing I had done (which, of course, was not putting her on hold and waking Richie up). He had met her the night before at a bar, didn't have her number but she had his. But what really bothered him was her hearing that he was "napping," which Richie called being seen in "the weakest light, a light that a real man would never want to be seen in."

If I get up at five in the morning to piss, I always hear him up strolling through the flat in his Allen A underwear, his shoes and socks on, the shower going all night because the strumming on the tub relaxes him, marking time until the first gray beeping of the horns and it starts all over again--the phone calls, the appointments, the working lunches. Sometimes, instead of going back to sleep, I stay up with him and watch it get light and smoke a lot of cigarettes and maybe go out to Riker's for coffee and sit there until the Barnard girls come in for breakfast. We'd talk about when we were young and girlfriends and playing ball and all the unbelievable things we did.

I swing around. My pants are on the floor and I pull them over the thermals. Richie, satisfied that I'm up, goes downstairs to check the mail. On my table an ashtray is overturned on Chapter Three of a novel I started when I moved in here. My latest page is forming a permanent bend in the broken down Royal portable that I work on. Several keys don't work right and a couple of others are missing entirely, the "v" and the "f." Lance Blatt sounds silly saying " uck you." It's in Chapter Three that Lance discovers he is the hero of my novel. That was quite a shock to him because in three chapters he hadn't lit up a cigarette or even walked across the room. At least *I* can walk across the room and here I go, into the kitchen and the cold linoleum floor. One of these days: slippers.

"Why, good morning," Alex says, exhaling with exaggerated boredom.

"Yeah, sure, good morning."

"He got *me* up first. I never even heard of Laura Longstreet."

"That's odd. She's one of the two or three most obscure people in the world."

His head falls back to the frieze of equations strung out on the long yellow legal pad he always uses.

Someday Alex will Invert the Matrix and become the only human in history to find a relationship between prime numbers. Sticky dust on top of the fridge.

I ask Alex how the casserole is. He says, "Standard Kovak."

There's a short foyer that leads into what used to be a darkroom. Richie and Marty sold most of the equipment for last June, July and August's rent and utilities but the long black drapes are still up, covering all of the walls and windows. Marty is snoring hideously. On the edge of the other couch is a female type that I don't know, brushing lint off her basic black.

"Hi," she says.

"Hi."

"Are you one of Marty's roommates?"

"I'm more of a freeloader buddy of Richie's."

"It's so dark in here."

"It used to be a darkroom."

"Oh, that's right. Marty makes movies."

"That's the line he gives all of his girlfriends."

"Does he have a lot of girlfriends?"

"Tons. But he's only interested in seducing them, and then gets rid of them, well, almost instantaneously."

She smiles. She thinks I'm kidding.

"What a big place."

"It's just that we're so small. What airline do you work for?"

"I don't work for an airline."

"What hospital do you work at?"

"St. Luke's. How did you know I was a nurse?"

"Well, you said you weren't a stewardess so you must be a nurse. My name's Mel."

"I'm Charlotte."

I notice her shoes on the snare drum. She looks too and we both smile. I think she digs me.

"Could you eat something?"

"Yes, actually."

"Come with me."

I walk back toward the kitchen and Charlotte follows, a spring boinging as she rises. She's just a tiny thing with short hair like a helmet. Marty the Satyr consorts only with nurses and stewardesses. Astoria, Long Island City, Whitestone, Rockville Center, they dig Kahlil Gibran, Edna St. Vincent Millay, Rona Jaffe. On their walls are bullfight posters, Dali's *Crucifixion*, passages from *The Razor's Edge* neatly typewritten on onionskin. They eat Hostess cupcakes, shave their bellies, send studio cards...

"Alex, would you ladle her some of that?"

The Well of Loneliness, cha cha records in wrought-iron record stands. Alex draws a southpaw star in the margin and looks up. Charlotte says hello and Alex,

39

trying to be civil, lifts his six and a half feet from the chair like a bandage slowly taken off after an operation. I dig Charlotte's legs. Even in bare feet she's got the great calf and diagonal shadow. In the light I see she has that early morning mongoloid look but it's good to know she never looks worse than this. It strikes me as the ideal way to begin an acquaintance.

Through the darkroom again, Marty still snoring like an idiot, down the long hallway past the living room where Norman, chain-smoking, is listening to Ray Charles low on the hi-fi, smoke all around him like gnats around carrion. *How's the steak Norman?...Oh man everything tastes like Chesterfields.* Norman's another one of Richie's charity cases. He's always scribbling stuff down in this thick notebook. Usually conversations that we're all having in the living room where he's always dug in on the couch he sleeps on. You have to watch what you say because Norman will write it all down in his notebook. He's either sitting on the couch scribbling his fanny off in a cocoon of smoke, or sitting on the couch listening to Ray Charles records—in a cocoon of smoke. Norman's got a 23-inch waist. Every once in a while one of us goes over to check his pulse. He slept in his shoes. He doesn't salt his eggs. If Norman could fly, he wouldn't.

Down the final hallway past the closet that has no door. Alex threw it out the window during Richie's Halloween party. He was demonstrating a burial at sea. In the bathroom I smell Norman's recent visit. Yes, I even know what everyone's bowel movement smells like in this pad. But Norman's isn't really that bad. A soft warm odor and smoky from his cigarette. That's what I smelled when I went into the bathroom right after my father, ashes in the sink and the New York Post on the floor.

Opening the cabinet in search of a blade, I make my way through the array of Marty's ointments, lotions, sprays and greasy jars with black hairs sticking to them. Yesterday was Thursday so it's what?--fourteen days since I've been out of the apartment. Or is it twenty-one days? Yeah, three Fridays ago. Maybe. It's either early December or mid-December. And the time I went out before that I found that Kennedy was our new President.

I shave down, re-lather, then shave up. I always shave the top lip first, then the chin, then the neck, then the right cheek, then the left cheek. Always. A little whitehead, let's call it a blemish, between the eyebrows. Marty's Aqua-Velva. I ought to come on to Charlotte. Just for the drill. I'm a reflection of the mirror. If there were no mirrors in the world men would walk around with crooked sideburns. I'm not handsome. No gainsaying that. Low cheekbones, small mouth. Better that way. Easier to identify with.

In the shower I work the nooks and crannies, scrub my funky cleft at the tailbone, expunge vagina-esque odors from my belly-button, wash the three-piece set (working in a brief auto-erotic intermezzo), and scrape dead skin from the bottom of my feet. I remember the day in the bathtub years ago when I discovered my asshole. I felt like the first person to circumnavigate his

41

body. I'm doing a Rodgers and Hart medley, singing *Where or When* at a ridiculously fast tempo, scatting maniacally. I segue to *Falling in Love with Love*, first in 3/4, then 4/4, then a slow, soulful *She Was too Good to Me*. If I started all over again I'd be a jazz singer.

I like a lot of towels. If I really am going outside and dealing with The Corner I better get mentally prepared. I just pitched a perfect game in the World Series, and broke a scoreless tie in the bottom of the ninth with a tape-measure solo shot, then fucked Princess Margaret in the dugout. Tonight I'm sitting in with the MJQ at Birdland.

Walking back down the hall. Ray Charles still low but audible. *Tell me how do you feel when your baby's lovin' your best friend?* Raelets: *I want to know. I want to know.* The phone rings just as I walk by it.

"Hello."

"Could I speak to Alex?"

"I'm afraid Alex has gone out. May I take a message?"

"I know he's there."

"You *know* he's here."

"That's correct."

"Well, I can't top that."

Through the darkroom, banging my toe against a box of reels. Charlotte has parted the drapes and is trying to get Marty up. My father used to rub my belly in slow circles and I'd wake up like a fluorescent bulb. Charlotte's handiwork is uninspired. You have to love someone to wake him up. One of her stockings has a huge run, sensualizing her little legs. In the kitchen Richie is reading a letter from his mother to Alex. Alex is reading *The Calculus of Finite Differences*.

"For you."

"Who is it?"

"Jane."

"Why didn't you--?"

"I did."

Alex lumbers off, mumbling and scratching his chest horizontally. Richie never stopped reading the letter. On the envelope, postmarked Maplewood, N.J., she addresses it to Richard Kovak, a worm in the Big Apple.

"...I told the milkman that in all the years I've purchased their dairy prod--"

"We praise the trumpets of the lieutenant."

"Dig this."

"Don't read the letter."

"'Me and Mrs. Roth are finally speaking again. We played bridge last Thursday and she apologized for calling me a bad partner. When I—'"

"So *that's* where you get it."

"Get what?"

I sit at the kitchen table and sniff his casserole.

"I had one of those dreams. It scared me. I died."

"You're supposed to wake up before you die."

"Everybody was chasing me and I wound up in the men's room and then I had to take a shit, which is more than Lance Blatt has ever had to do, but I didn't have any money so I tried climbing over the pay-toilet but I fell and went down the toilet. Head first."

"Couldn't afford the pay-toilet, huh? What a loser...let me finish telling you about last night."

"Give me some of that funny looking stuff."

I didn't mention the part about my father. He serves up his infamous casserole, making sure that nary a drop defiles his black cashmere coat which he will not take off until the apartment warms up.

"You recall Mrs. Hamilton?"

"Of course not."

"Mrs. Hamilton, whom you pretend not to remember, is a dear friend of Laura's and also happens to be, get this, the great-granddaughter of Joseph Pulitzer."

"Too much garlic. And the raisins were a big mistake."

"She'll put up her fifty thousand on two conditions."

"Or was it *two* thousand on *fifty* conditions?"

"One, that's it's not part of the first hundred thou, and two, that her summer-stock niece gets to play Faith. Perfect casting, don't you think? Which reminds me that I've got to be downtown by eleven to see

Arnold Klopman. He's the key to Roland Beckstein. The kicker being, if Universal likes the distribution deal, Rottman, Bottomly & Kahn will put up their seventy grand whereupon Mrs. Hamilton's fifty grand swings into action. Then Allied will approve the budget of $195,000 and shooting begins in the spring..."

"I won't let them shoot you, Richie."

Marty shuffles in barefoot, his eyes squinty and his teeth clenched because he thinks it's virile to wake up in a bad mood. Richie keeps on bebbing.

"...I just have to fearlessly confront the milieu...I got Longstreet interested again, Beckstein in the bag, Antonio Silver in the second lead, and I got Wilson Getz telling me a week ago on the phone that he'd like to direct a movie."

Marty shakes the coffee pot, pats it, pats it again, pats it again and burns himself. Marty and Richie are Rosebud Productions which is basically Richie's screenplay, *The Vandals*, a noir thing about how we all lie, cheat and steal. It's really good, actually, and I must not be the only one who thinks so because he's got people throwing money at him on spec, operating money, front money, money for restaurant tabs, hotel tabs, etc. He is thus able to take on human detritus like me, Alex, and Norman. The thing that Marty's got going is that his father is president of Allegheny Chemical Savings and Loan. As an added bonus, he tosses Richie an occasional stewardess. I understand that Marty was an ace football player at Colgate, honorable mention All-East or some shit but now, five years later, he's already got that blustering alumni look, and a gut that he sees as a harbinger of success. He still wears his big hairy college ring as if that stuff still made a difference.

Marty starts shuffling back out of the kitchen with a cup in each hand but he filled both cups to the brim and the coffee trickles down, burning his fingers and splashing on the back of his hands. Now he's pissed. Charlotte sprints in to bail him out, taking her cup. This Charlotte is a keeper.

Richie presses his profane arms on Alex's long pages of notes. I stand up and announce, "I'm going out."

"Hm."

"That's the long and the short of it."

"I suppose you know what you're doing?"

"I think so. Yeah."

"It's a young idea. Quixotic."

"I guess."

"What about The Corner?"

"I'll just face it when it comes."

"I like that in a guy. Then what?"

"You know, nothing elaborate."

"Christian Science reading room, coffee at Bickford's...?"

"That's it. That kind of thing...I might call Margot."

"Need I remind you about the Christmas party tonight?"

"I guess you do need to. I'll probably miss it."

"You'll be missing a great party. Remember Ruthie? She runs a catering service and she owes me one. Why you might ask? Because I promised her the role of Faith's sexy younger sister. Of course, as you know, Faith doesn't have a sister but in a flash I realized that she *needs* one. For contrast. You get my drift?"

"I really think I do...If I see Margot I'll probably spend the night there."

"And if you don't see Margot?"

"Then I'll make up something else. I hate your parties, okay?"

Richie looks a little hurt by that. All right, I'm ungrateful. But he's a martyr, so we're even. No, we're not even. I resent him because I'm "in care of" him. He falls back on the chair as if the overcoat is exhausting him. He talks now about the crucial significance of his appointment with Klopman. Klopman is tight with Wilson Getz, who is probably the biggest theater director in New York at the moment. Richie says Getz suddenly is gaga to make a movie and is looking around for a suitable property. I'm dubious, okay? I try to imagine Richie Kovak, patriarch of the idle poor, up on the fortieth floor talking big money with these people. He's still wading through his mail. I get up quickly, full of purpose, and return to my room.

I put some new cardboard in both my shoes and get

dressed. As I dress I try to think of what I'll do outside and if I really will call Margot. It would be a stupid, destructive and selfish thing to do. I need a cigarette.

Marty and Charlotte are sitting on the floor, their backs against the couch. They're caught in the white morning light that knifes through the parted drapes. She stares at her palm like she's never seen it before and he hides behind his cigarette. Last night's juices dried and stinking up the joint.

"Why hello there, you two lovebirds. Is anyone smoking regular non-filtered?"

"I got a Winston. Take it or leave it."

As I'm thinking of a riposte, Charlotte, goddess of the machine, jumps up and says, "I've got Camels."

A female type who smokes Camels? Impressive.

"They're in my purse in the bathroom."

"I certainly didn't intend any inconvenience."

"No trouble at all."

"Very considerate of you, Charlotte."

She runs out. I love her legs, I want to marry her legs.

"Marty, thou hast committed fornication. But that was in another borough. And besides, the wench is a nurse."

"Goddam scrounge."

"Man, you have a Don Juan complex."

48

"It's better than you jerking off in the bathtub."

"You can't provoke me with indignities."

"Is it better or not?"

"Aesthetically, maybe."

"So it's better, right?"

Howie, satisfied with his edge in the argument, flicks his ash in the coffee cup, leans his head back against the couch, and stares at the ceiling. Alex is still on the phone as I walk to the hall closet for my coat, my father's coat that I took with me from Mercy Hospital in Miami. And his wallet. And his cool moonstone ring. And his watch that is rusting in my toilet kit. *Your father has expired.* I hate doctors. They can't even tell you that your father is dead.

Charlotte, returning, shows me the cigarettes and offers up the pack with a grin. One of them slides out and I catch it in the air but she tried to catch it too and we, like on the trapeze, lock pinkies. I exploit the moment with my A smile but she passes on it and does a one-eighty back to Howie on the floor.

A couple of weeks ago a few of us were sitting in a circle on the living room floor drinking wine. Richie, me, Marty and his girlfriend, a stewardess, natch, named Marla, two-three others. Marla, out of left field, picks up my hands and says, "Wow, you have beautiful hands."

That felt nice. Later when the rest of them had gone and it was just me and Richie finishing the jug, he says to me, "Did you pick up on that thing when Marla said you have beautiful hands?"

"What thing?"

"She was trying to make Marty jealous by giving you some juice there...I mean come on, obviously you don't have beautiful hands."

Now I don't know whether I have beautiful hands or not.

Alex sees that I'm ready and gestures for me to wait up. Once Alex fell asleep talking to Jane. I heard *clunk* and, when I turned, Alex was slumped in the chair and the receiver was on the floor, Jane yelling "Alex, are you there?"

"...all right, all right...*yes*...in about an hour..."

He holds the receiver by the scruff of the neck and stares at it before hanging up.

"Thwarted Mathematician Strangles Career Girl... you can't just *like* Jane. She feels insulted."

"I'm outta here."

"You got subway money?"

"I got a buck. I'll break it downstairs."

"Let me get my shoes."

Between tracks of Ray Charles I hear Norman back to sleep. Norman has a severe Brooklyn accent. There's a numismatics magazine called Coin World which he pronounces Kern Woild.

In the living room, monumental against the wide morning window, stands The Black Rook, arms akimbo, staring across the Hudson, consulting his oracle, the ALCOA sign spread across the Palisades.

I knew the face would discolor when the glass broke. Then the rust came to the gold numbers and the hands. I should've taken better care of it. It had stopped at ten minutes before eleven. I knew the insides were rotten but I wound it anyway. And then the second-hand began moving like a nervous insect. Sent a chill through me.

Richie turns from the wide window and tilts his head as though Alex and I are simply adorable.

"Now Mel, don't forget to share your spending money with Alex."

He heard. Walking by the darkroom, we wave goodbye to Marty and Charlotte. She waves back but Marty is still staring at the ceiling.

Down the elevator whose functioning is triannually guaranteed by G. Gormley. His six signatures are tall and thin. Alex digs Charlotte. He finds her "attractive," a word he doesn't usually use.

"What do *you* think?" he says.

"Yeah, if you're into young vibrant heterosexual women."

"She's a nurse."

"She also smokes Camels."

"Here at St.Luke's, in the eye bank. She's kinda short."

"I prefer small girls. They make me feel I have a big penis."

"Charlotte has one quality that Jane doesn't have."

"What's that?"

"I just met Charlotte."

"Yeah, Jane sure is deficient in that area."

"You can say that again."

Through the lobby, we walk with the grain of the long rubber carpet. Even though I'm, as my mother used to say, "a six-footer" (*Melvin, stand up and show your Uncle Nathan how tall you are…How's the weather up there?...Oh I don't know haha…*), next to Alex I feel diminutive. He's built like Humphrey Pennyworth but he walks like Howdy Doody, his nervous system working only to detect doorways, dashboards and all the other unsung horrors of The Macrocosm. Alex's idea of fun is to sit in a comfortable chair.

Outside it's snowing lightly, like powdered sugar. Who calls me cruller? This gray vacant stretch of boulevard is my last chance to escape across the wilderness. I chicken out every time I think about doing it. Soon through the cupcake trees of Riverside Park I see the boulevard roil and a rumble of movement. It's water. The Hudson River.

As we approach 116th the wind starts whipping

around The Corner, scaring the snow. We hit the left turn, pow, and hunch in unison, screaming, denouncing the galaxy.

My life passes before me in a sickening montage. How could I have spent that summer translating the complete works of Luke Short into Coptic? To have borne *fardels* only to perish on this barren heath in the full bloom of obscurity. I don't deny the obscurity. I'm a piece of coal on a black rug in a dark room at midnight. But I glint, here and there.

Alex yells, "I'm hit."

I think of positive images. Anita Ekberg sitting on my face, reciting the *Rubaiyat*. I find, from watching the grain of the cement below me, that we're gaining whole squares of sidewalk at a time. Let's bring our boys home for Purim.

Up on Broadway we hang a right and the wind suddenly dies down. The cold is goading everyone. Students are bundled and full of purpose. The snow is in the way, annoying the air. Everyone grimaces. Even *I* grimace.

Alex informs me that "the earth is an oblate spheroid with a 3% eccentricity." I stop in front of the Chock Full O' Nuts and tell him to wait outside. There isn't enough room in there for him anyway. I walk in and give my dollar to the tall skinny cashier with Irma on her name-card. I've had this dollar stuffed in my left coat pocket since the last time I left the apartment. I sold a book, *Nine Great Tragedies*. At approximately eleven cents a tragedy. The scalloped counter is packed. In the mirror I have something going with a pale long-faced girl wearing a SANE button. I press my teeth together trying to accentuate my cheekbones, such as they are. She's eating cream cheese on date-nut bread and when she chews her temples ripple. Irma gives me four quarters. One last glance in the mirror. The girl with the SANE button loves me. My teeth hurt.

I find Alex by the curb, staring across the street to College Walk. Now we both stand there staring. His physics and math professors thought Alex was a rising star but he got bored with the classes and walked away, deciding to work on his own. Just a boy and his matrix.

"Fucking A cold," I say, just to snap him out of it. We've all got to snap out of it.

"Where you going?"

"I might wind up at Margot's."

"I thought that was over with."

I give him two quarters.

"All I need's fifteen cents."

"Keep it."

"Maybe I should. Last time we got in a fight I stormed out but I had to go back and ask her for subway fare."

"Rookie mistake. You should always ask for return

subway fare *as soon as you get there*."

"Thanks for the tip."

He tries a smile but can't sustain it. I watch him cross the street against the light to the subway station. We're in a glass paperweight, the kind that snows when God shakes it. Soon just Alex's blond head and shoulders as he walks in the door, suddenly with everyone, going somewhere.

Alex also grew up in Milford. He knows the drill, the big city/small town axis. I think of all the times I took that train back and forth, from the dinky railroad station in Milford (pop. 5,000) to Grand Central Station in the Babe Ruth of cities (pop. 8 million). Waiting at the Milford station for the 3:57, sitting there staring at the big lumber yard. The Laurelton Hall girls after school, standing on the platform jabbering. *During chemistry Sister Eleanor left the room and Valerie told JoAnn D'Alessandro that Bobby Wickersham was going to take her to the dance on Friday, so I said for your information Bobby asked* me *to go to the dance, so she says he told me that the only reason he asked you was because you blew him two weeks ago at Gulf Beach, so I said that's a cheap lie I only jerked him off, so she says you're so stupid that's the same thing*. C'mon, Valerie doesn't know the difference between a blowjob and a handjob?

The early train is the hardest. As the commuters get on at Norwalk, Westport, Stamford, Greenwich, Cos fucking Cob, they talk loud. They don't notice you. They have their literature, their myths. And you know you haven't. You're not a sociological phenomenon. You live too far up the line for that, beyond the commute, beyond John Cheever. Watching the lonely Westchester depots, Rye, Port Chester, the railyards, the billboards and then the Bronx where you were born, you feel your greatness rising and you welcome it. Alone on a train you'd better be great. You go through Harlem and think about politics and how nothing's ever going to change ever ever ever. But even that doesn't matter because you don't have much time left. When the train goes underground at 79th Street, the panic starts. Your last joke on everyone is when they all get up to wait in the aisle. You know it'll be eight more minutes. You sit there feeling like a New Yorker. At Grand Central you walk by the information kiosk and everything starts getting remote. All you ever read or said or thought or did. An empty cup. You stop and get a Times and flip through a Life magazine because you know there's only one more set of doors and you don't want to walk through them. When you step onto 42nd Street you feel a little crazy, like someone's watching you from the 40th floor of the Chrysler building. He loses you for a moment in the crowd but then he finds you again, jaywalking toward the library. You get smaller and smaller walking along Bryant Park and when he loses you the next time he can't find you anymore.

Chapter Two

In the thumbs of the street. I'm a figure placed for scale in an architectural model. The weather's ridiculous. A center of culture and all that. It's about ten degrees and the wind is vicious. In front of Salter's asthmatic bookstore, the stacks all the way up to the high ceiling. *Sociophysics and the Byronic Moment, Metier and Meta-ego: The Pre-Kantian Sources of Pluralistic Monism.* An examination of some notes toward an introduction to an inquiry into prefatory remarks with index, foreword, table of contents, epigraph, acknowledgements, frontispiece, dedication, bibliography, appendix, glossary, prologue, epilogue, colophon, blurbs, errata, addenda. Gutenberg's assistant, Fritz, stole the wrong brain! Readable, literate, makes a lovely gift. A dinosaur of books. And at its feet, ant-people in listless worship. And asthma has one little vowel on either side, like bookends propping up the consonants, asphyxiating them. *The Politics of Politics*.

The shoemaker looks warm and busy in his long green smock. Reminds me of my father in his tailor shop on snowy mornings. It'd be freezing when we opened up but after the oil burner kicked in it got real cozy, a radio whispering news, music and a warning to motorists. Not much business. Just a few regulars. Mario the cop would need to get a button sewed back on his uniform. Mrs. Van Arsdale, who looked like Nina Foch, might come in to put a Community Concerts poster in the window. *We hope to get Andre*

Kostelanetz back again next year. And the guy who sold tailoring supplies. He was Zero Mostel's brother. Soon after opening I'd walk up the street to Jake's to get him his coffee-and. Then we'd chitchat over the New Haven Journal-Courier about current events. He refused to believe that Alger Hiss was guilty. So neither did I. He was a lefty in Poland but after coming to America he bought the whole myth and became a solid Democrat. He wanted me to go to law school and do good things for the needy. I guess he never thought *I'd* be the needy one.

Through Riker's window the pale Barnard girls at their morning meal. They wear polo coats, trench coats, and big coats with glossy logs for buttons. Columbia is the sultan and Barnard is the seraglio. On the windowsill are textbooks. *The Age of Romanticism.* Heck of an age. A couple of math books and a slide rule. I knew a guy, seventy-five years old, taught history at UConn, spent seventy years of his life in school.

A: Identify:

1) Massenet
2) Mazarin
3) Massena
4) Mazzini
5) Masereel
6) Masaryk
7) Mazeroski

B: 1) What unique distinction is attributed to Sir

Goodwin "Goodie" Van Choc-Straw?

2) Name the Norwegian diplomat who said, "I suppose so."

3) Write a short essay on God. Be specific. Cite examples.

It's starting to hail. Broadway is capsizing. Across the street seems miles away. It's really pissing me off. I slip and slide, trying to remember why, after three weeks, I came out into all of this. Somewhere, at this exact moment, off the California coast, the world's most voluptuous woman is diving off a sixty-foot yacht. Up the rope ladder, rhinestoned by the sun, she climbs on deck and stands like an amazon queen, arms akimbo, hips and shoulders heaving in wanton rhythms. She undoes her bikini, lies down on a long leopard-skin cushion and oils herself with attar of African lustroot. She throbs and pulsates. Her legs snap open and closed. She's begging this older distinguished guy, played by Louis Calhern, who sits in his swiveling orthopedic deckchair with a sweating daiquiri in his hand. He's thinking, damn, this is the greatest thing since the Dodgers moved to LA.

The Flamingo canopy is flipping and flapping. As I walk through the door my glasses steam up. At the counter I take them off, peel a napkin from the dispenser and with thumb and index finger wipe-dry my lenses. As I sit down, with these same two versatile fingers, I thwart the presumptuous career of my underwear. I don't have a toothache.

The waitress' blood-red fingernail polish is a bit

much this early in the morning. She's skinny as hell, veins all over the place. What kind of ghoul is this to encounter in an eating establishment? I give her my truck-stop routine, blowing into my fist, rubbing my hands together and then quickly, as if it's a waste of time talking about it: "Make it hot."

Sitting to my left is Joan Crawford's stuntwoman, cutting her eggs with a fork *and knife*. An order of toast pops up. Somebody better get on it. The waitress returns and bangs the big mug down in front of me so that some coffee splashes over the side, rolls down to the counter, then quickly forms a ring around the mug. Behind that the check discreetly face down, a corner folded for easy pickup.

Sitting to my right is a fat guy, really huge, reading the Inquiring Photographer: Do You Believe in Love at First Sight? Fearing that the slightest glance at him is some kind of indictment, I look into my napkin but sense him there like a tree you walk under. His nose and mouth and eyes are like the bruises on a honeydew melon. From the fragmentary headline, a liaison has been disclosed. The toast is still popped up in the toaster and is no doubt cold by now. C'mon, you gotta get right on that toast. I pick up my hot cup without using the handle because I'm so leathery and spontaneous. The coffee's weak. I should complain but I'm much too manly for that. When mom made the coffee too weak my father used to say, "You can see Paris through this."

The lights are off and it's pretty dark in here.

Probably a power failure. *Why are you reading in such a bad light?...Oh pop, you get used to it...You get used to hanging if you hang long enough.* He had a million of 'em. Even a stopped clock is right twice a day. Figures don't lie and liars don't figure. On the average, over his whole life, you could count on him for about two or three epigrams per hour, sitting at the sewing machine, changing a bobbin, with the red pin cushion on one of my bicycle clips manacled to his wrist.

I have a little argument with myself over who's going to pay the check, *You paid last time*, and walk over to the cashier, a worldly looking fellow with a cigar. When I put the change in my overcoat pocket I feel a key.

Outside it's become the worst day I've ever seen and it's not even ten o'clock. Past Gristedes where the mayonnaise is on sale. I let it snow in my mouth. When I was in high school, marauding through the corridors, smoking in the bathrooms where I searched with my voice for the perfect pitch from the high glossy walls, Miss Peckham, wearing the world like a swastika, told me that I still had a chance to be somebody if I ever decided to apply myself. I did apply myself to basketball but I didn't make the high school team— twice. The second time I was the last guy cut. Damn right I was disappointed. During the third quarter of the JV game the whole varsity squad would descend the bleachers in an epic wake of parents, buddies, girlfriends, and in full view, walk single-file to the locker room, carrying their gym bags, wearing maroon-and-white warm-up jackets, loafers and white socks.

The hail cauterizes my face and the wind blows me into Walgreen's. The phones are all the way in back. I walk by the Kaopectate, the Unguentine, the Maalox. Come Preparation H, come loaf with me. Depilatories, suppositories, I sing of the mutuality of us. Empirin, Ace bandage, Vaseline, Humphrey's 11 additionally. I subsume you all, each of the other, thus. I sit in a damp booth and dial carefully. A wrong number would sabotage my exchequer.

"Good morning, Bender and Fry."

"Miss Jurgenson, if you would."

"Thank you...Miss Jurgenson's line is busy."

"I'll hold."

"All right, sir...I'm ringing...I'm ringing...Miss Jurgenson's line is still busy, sir. Would you like to call back?"

"No."

"Who's calling, please."

"Mr. Poe."

"And with whom are you associated?"

"Evinrude."

"Thank you, sir, I'll try again...I'm ringing...I'm sorry. Her phone is still busy."

"That's perfectly fine. I'll wait. Yeoman work, by the way."

"She may be a while. Would you rather call back in a bit?"

"It's my last dime."

"Ha ha, all right, sir, as you wish."

Don't laugh. If I had this dime in my dream last night it would've saved my life. Scratched on the brown pebble-grain wall, Gordon's love for Brenda seems sincere. Below that, "Call AC 3-7494, she'll suck it." An obvious comma split but what can you do?

"Media, Miss Jurgenson."

"Hi, Margot."

"Oh."

"Exactly."

"How are you?"

"I really don't know."

"I kind of miss you."

"Ha, great line."

"Are you about to apologize for staying away for two months without a word."

"I apologize."

"Okay, you don't have to get maudlin about it."

"I thought you'd rather I stayed away."

"I guess I miss being miserable."

"I'm not feeling very guilty at the moment."

"I didn't mean it that way, I don't think."

"Yeah. It's hard to talk on the phone."

"Off the phone, too."

"An argument can be made that I shouldn't have called."

"If an argument can be made, you'll make it. Why did you?"

Why did I? Because I love you. Easy now.

"I guess I'm horny…Some prose for the groundlings."

"Do you want to see me tonight?"

"Yes."

"Come for dinner."

"Okay."

"Pretty bad storm, huh?"

"Yeah."

"I'll be home around six. You still have the key?"

"Yeah."

"Go over early if you want. Read something."

"Maybe I will."

"All right."

"Later."

Why don't they make coffins out of old phone booths. A few bedlamites, ducking in out of the storm, hang around the paperback racks, looking for the dirty parts. *Simulacrum and Verisimilitude in Byzantine*

Iconography, Clovis and the Merovingian Ecstasy, Dinah Won't You Blow: Psychosexuality in American Folk Music. We all track in the snow and it melts disconsolately on the green tile floor. There's Leo straddling his briefcase, checking out a Commentary. He's never been seen without his briefcase. He wears earmuffs and a knitted cap. A red scarf hangs out of his coat pocket to the floor. I want his scarf. I want his earmuffs, too. Leo's wife, Lisa, is one of those born-and-bred East 80s chicks with shiny skin like from cold cream. One night I'm over at their pad hanging out with Leo and out of left field she's got to show me her new Teflon frying pan. Leo says, "Lisa, for god's sake," but she drags it down from the wall and explains how it fries without grease because it has a non-stick surface. Oooh I guess we're now ready for the apocalypse. She asks me if she can make me an egg to show me. I say no thanks, so she asks Leo. He says, "Lisa, for god's sake, it's just a frying pan." "Couldn't you eat just one little egg?" she asks him, and plop an egg is frying on the Teflon pan and she shows me the special spatula she uses. She hands me the spatula *so I can see how easy the egg flips over.* I'm standing there with the spatula in my hand. Then she remembers that Leo likes sunnyside up so she asks Leo if he'd mind "just so Mel can see how it flips the egg." Leo is ready to vomit either way so he says sure and she nods excitedly to me and I flip the egg. I'm here to tell the world that the egg did not stick. She serves it with a cloth napkin, pepper mill, the whole bit and there's Leo actually eating the fucking egg. And not even the way he likes it.

I hang a sharp right to avoid being seen. Leo's cool but I doubt my ability to make small talk. It's this skill I used to have. I try slipping out the side door but he sees me.

"Mel?"

"Oh, hey, man, how's it going?"

"Not bad. What about you?"

"Oh why bother others with one's own wretched misfortune."

"What are you doing up so early in this weather?"

"Actually, I'm looking for a job."

"Hm. How's Richie?"

"Oh busy with the movie."

"Have his backers come through yet?"

"Nah. You know. The money's coming in Monday. It's just a big runaround."

"That's show biz, huh?"

"So how's school? You taking your anals?"

"I decided to take them in the summer. I'm just working on my thesis."

"*The Deltaic Economy after Diocletian.*"

"Great memory."

"I guess you know that Egyptology is a pseudo-science."

"Of course."

"In that case, why don't you buy me a beer."

"I wish I had time but I've got to run to the library."

"I can dig that."

"You need money?"

"No no no."

Pulling out his wallet. Fuck.

"Here, let me give you a couple of bucks."

"No. Absolutely. Thanks anyway. Please…"

"Come on, I know how it is."

No you don't, Leo. *Oh pop, I'll be okay. Don't worry so much.*

He opens my hand and slips the stiff bills into it. As I touch them, the stiffness and the chalkiness, it seems like more than it is. It seems like a lot of money.

"Thanks, Leo."

"It's nothing. What are you talking about?"

"I'll pay you back soon."

The money's coming in Monday. I have to get away. I feel like a burr on his sleeve.

"Well, I'll pick up a Times, look through the want ads."

"Stop by the Viking sometime and say hello. Lisa asks about you."

"I will. Regards to Lisa."

The blind newsman on the corner sits in his hut with a dog on his lap keeping each other warm. I buy a Times and suddenly want to know what's happening in the world. Mincing across the street, I fold the paper under my coat. The subway beneath me is breaking for the 110th Street stop. Its roar thins into a screech and steam rises through the esplanade grating. My feet are a disgrace, making squeegy sounds, and since the new cardboard is already defunct I'm forced to walk heel and toe. My feet feel like grilled corn muffins. I crash through the doors of the Gold Rail and make my way to the bar. I hear Andy's voice but I can't see him.

"Well, lookee here."

"Got a napkin?"

"We got everything."

From behind the bar Andy gets a couple of oversized ones and puts them in my hand. I order a Schlitz on tap and wipe the steam off my lenses. He takes his time with the head, tap on tap off tap on tap off. I pull one of the singles out of my pocket. I shouldn't give him this dollar bill. I should keep it pressed in a big dictionary and save it for my children. Andy sets the mug down, plucks the bill from my fingers, rings it up and leaves me with the coins of Judas.

I walk over to the high-back booth and shake out my coat. Huge rafters overhead, pewters on a long shelf, gothic lettering and other corny hofbrau bits. There's one old woman and three old men at the bar, all of them sitting sideways, looking out at the brazen day. They look and look and look. Expressionless, like fish heads.

The Cold War rages on the front page of the Times. Not to mention the hot wars, wars of revolution-- Algeria, Vietnam, everywhere, actually. But I'm used to this. The year I was born Hitler was openly killing Jews, Mussolini was running amuck, the Spanish Civil War began (with the fascists supported by Hitler and Mussolini), and Japan was revving up for the World War that began three years later. It's now 15 years since the war ended but not much has changed except the dramatis personae. If I wanted to I could feel disillusioned, sold out by the older generation, thrill-seeking and without values because I live in an immoral world. That would be terrific.

Trespassing through the Business-Finance section. I see that Arthur L. McPhee has been named New England District Manager of Greeley Enterprises. He looks like my father, the way his smile sends semi-circles from the corners of his mouth. And the V-shape hairline, too. Your picture in the paper. A complete accident.

On the screened-in porch in Milford, he used to play pinochle with Charlie Sabloff, Manny Rosenthal, and Dave Berman, the crickets kibitzing, and me, allowed to sit near the table if I promised not to say a word. I think of his big hands dealing the cards, the hands that held me like a trophy, and the Pall Malls burning in the ashtray, and his lungs choked by two little vowels.

The pinochle ritual was elaborate. If a player to my father's right led a card to him, say a queen of hearts, my father might say, "Queen of hearts, that's a smart card," and when he discarded, the next player would embellish. "Oh yes, a very very smart card." Then the fourth player would have to resolve it with something like "Too smart for its own good" as he put a king on it to win the trick. The pace was slow, deliberate, with all of the dialogue muttered off-handedly, their eyes on their cards, rarely looking up until the hand was over. The post-mortem between deals while someone was shuffling was a succinct analysis.

"I thought you had clubs."

"I thought *you* had clubs."

The day writhes outside. I look and look and look. Margot is as good as it gets, female-wise, but foisting myself on her wouldn't be fair.

One night between sets at the Five Spot, I said, "Love is a band-aid."

She says, "Love is the cut...You're just afraid."

"Of what?"

"Of relationships ending, leaving you lonely like you felt after your parents died...I feel sorry for you."

"Knock that shit off."

I hate someone feeling sorry for me. Unless they absolutely insist.

"I just want you to know I understand," she says.

"All right, don't smother me with understanding."

I remember once going into my parents' bedroom to look for something. They weren't around. I opened the bottom drawer and found this booklet that had words I didn't know: zygote, gestation, fallopian. There were diagrams that looked like roadmaps in the body where eggs dropped and sperm swam, where glands secreted and life connected. In that same drawer I also found yellowing photos from their vacations at Bear Mountain ("till Bear Mountain dresses" in the four corners of the autograph book). Mom and dad and Uncle Nathan and Aunt Lena who had six husbands and Mrs. Greenspan whose son became an eye doctor as well as the object of intra-mishpucha reverence (*Eli Greenspan is a regular Einstein*) and all the others in their nutty bathing suits, posing the way people don't pose anymore. All of them frozen in the bottom drawer, yellowing. My parents were Jazz Age immigrants who came from Poland to the New World and begat a daughter, who was everything you'd want in a daughter, and a son, a classic myopic fuck-up who can't get out of his own way.

My mother was the youngest of thirteen children. What if her parents decided to stop at twelve? Which would've been reasonable. She wouldn't have existed and I wouldn't have existed. But I do exist. I do.

What am I doing in such a depressing place with all of these taxidermied people looking and looking and looking? I finish off the beer in one pleasure-pain swallow, drop the mug off on the bar and give Andy a wordless military salute. I walk out full of purpose, going home to Ipswich, Massachusetts where I live with my wife and three children. En route to the subway entrance. I'm being triple-teamed but I throw a few baffling head fakes and break loose for a leaping, spinning jump shot from the corner. Swish. Each time I score the opposing coach calls time out. How're we gonna stop Montrose? The cheerleaders worship me and why shouldn't they? I'm smooth, I'm varsity.

Downstairs at the 110th Street station, through the turnstile. The people on the platform, steam out of their mouths, walk in jagged circles trying to keep warm. One guy in a salt-and-pepper overcoat is whistling *Thou Swell*. More Rodgers and Hart! This inspires me to mentally superimpose a walking bass line over his flute-like whistle. He can't hear me but we're swinging. Upstaged by the wheezing roar of the subway, I go right to the coda--and gosh but you're witty and swell and so pretty and grand: bit-it-in-dwee. The cymbals spread, then narrow and ba-dump just as my foot steps onto the train. I'll sit across from her.

None of that neo-realist 241st Street-White Plains squalor, or the 145th Street-Lenox Avenue eyesore. This is the serene 242nd Street-Van Courtland Park. Warm, lit-up red lettering, powder-blue tile, leatherette seats. No crime, no grime, this is hip public transit. By 96th I'm mellow, 33 1/3, wanting a scarf but reconciled.

She shaved her big handsome legs this morning. Along the ridge of the tibia are three little cuts, like red

72

ants. A sequined M on her purse. She *looks* like a Marie. Marie Gagliardi. Her coat is open, revealing some impressive cleavage. Probably from the Bronx. Seeing her lawyer about the breach-of-promise case. Friday night she goes to the neighborhood movie where they advertise the candy counter during intermission. But she closes the coat now and keeps her hand there, playing with the extra-large top button. Nice, shapely, hairy, milky, Etruscan woman. Downy sideburns and open pores. Formidable, women are. They scare me. Breasts, brassieres, menstruation. What a fantastic contraption. Nipples, garter belts, ganglia, tendrils, flagella. They numb you with their lust. She looks at me. I look away. I look at her. She looks away. She looks at me. I look away. I look at her. She looks away. I smile now, turning her off completely as she rises at 50th to wait by the door for her Times Square stop. Eight streets she stands.

Miss Subways looks like Ella Raines. She enjoys swimming, bowling, knitting and heavy petting. Next to her, a public notice warning first graders to avoid rapists if it's at all possible, with an unbelievably hack drawing of a kid being offered candy by a swarthy Steve Cochran type. Despite lousy peripheral vision I notice that Marie, still waiting for her stop, is actually looking at me. My first thought: Do I go with one of my famous tongue movements? Certainly I'll accentuate my cheekbones, even though my teeth still hurt since the Chock Full O' Nuts incident. I won't belabor this. I'm going to be forthright and spontaneous or forget about it entirely. The only question that remains is, do

I have the confidence to throw my breaking ball with a three-and-oh count. I turn slowly and look at her.

She looks away. Gives me her broad ardent back as an afterthought.

At Times Square she steps onto the platform and divides the crowd waiting to get on. They flood the car, jockeying for seats and filling the aisles. I watch her and wonder if she really has ended all attempts to communicate with me. Life is a B film, the world is a condemned movie lot, we're all extras with only one line--and we blow it. If she looks back I'll follow her to that lawyer who's extorting her, drill him on the spot and move away with her to Costa Rica where we'll start a new life together. Until, of course, Fate catches up with us. Starring Victor Mature and Audrey Totter.

As she walks, her hair bounces. I'm about to give up on her when suddenly, without stopping, she turns her head *and looks at me*. I scramble up, knocking the Tribune out of this guy's hands, though I do take a millisecond to apologize, and bump into a mouton coat. Racing to the middle doors just as they're closing, I'm slowed down by a fucking suitcase so I leap sideways and stick in the doors, sandwiched in and not going anywhere. I get both arms in the space and try prying the doors but it's no go. I can keep them from closing but I can't open them and when I yell out for the conductor I lose the tension and the doors close on me. I kick the door and jam my big toe. Ow. I wait to see if the conductor heard me but the train starts moving and I go back to my seat, now occupied by the mouton coat. I bend over, looking through the window, and try to find her in the crowd. There she is at the foot of the stairs and she sees me. I wave at her. Marie, we both sort of tried, didn't we? But she just stares blankly at me. Lot's wife. The platform ends and suddenly I'm looking at my fatherless reflection in the window.

When I straighten up I hear some mumbling from the mouton coat and the guy with the Tribune too. He sort of brushes it off and refolds it, trying to show me that the damage I did was nearly irreparable.

"Lady, you're in my seat."

She hits me with an eyebrow number. Too outraged to utter, right?

"I don't even care," I tell her, "I just wanted you to know."

"Oh, did you?"

Now a full-on Jinx Falkenburg. Big ring on her middle finger. She's thinking, I'm not going to stoop to any public altercation. Oh look, the Tribune's going to show me.

"You stay put."

"I certainly intend to."

"He lost his seat. That's *his* problem."

How true, as Norman might say.

At the Sheridan Square station I walk up the stairs and turn up my collar. No top button. The second straight winter without a top button. Which would be okay with a scarf. The street is so dark there's a lamp on over the news-stand. The traffic down Seventh Avenue is processional. Cars crawl up to the stoplight, their rear ends fishtailing. Down Christopher Street people hunch toward me. Here comes this old woman with a babushka. When she walks past me I'm going to throw a vicious block on her, just nail her, springing the runner loose at midfield.

I turn into Bedford Street. My feet crunch the powdery snow which makes me shiver like scratching a blackboard. The parked cars tip toward the curb. Strange but there's nobody else on the street as far as I can see, narrowing down to Seventh Avenue. Like a Utrillo painting, no people and no car traffic, either. I'm looking for someone to see me walking to Margot's apartment.

I used to think I'd wind up in faculty housing--volatile, sensuous, dynamic, chain-smoking over my Henry Vaughn article, *Lyric Doubt and the Bardic Sensibility*. Making it with the muddy-complected Chaucerians, having them up to my pad for absinthe, one by one. And when I ran out of the Chaucerians, I'd start in on the Spenserians.

In front of Margot's building I wait a while. There is just the sound of the trapped wind swinging in the streets, hammocking back and forth, moaning the blues.

Chapter Three

Through the alley door and into a woolly silence, dark-wooded walls and a butterscotch rug flooding the floor. Walking up one flight I feel the bristles of the rug through the holes in my shoes. I prepare the key, pausing for my lenses to fully unsteam. Inside, the shades are down and the rooms are dark. I stand there listening to the hum of the silence. A feather I've found and don't know what to do with. I take off my damp coat and drape it around a chair.

Margot's place is always neat and tasty. The little Memlings on the wall, the cool cigarette urn on the coffee table. In the kitchen I explore the fridge, its light falling onto the floor. I spot some cottage cheese and get myself a spoon but upon opening the lid I find that several bacilli have pitched their tents. Bad luck for Mel. An apple instead and a chocolate graham. On top of the fridge is a tiny bit of scotch. I finish it off and look on the shelf under the sink but there isn't any more. No cigarettes either and I look everywhere--in her raincoat, in her other purse, in the drawers, closets, cabinets, on the shelves, tables, counters. Even in the cool cigarette urn. No cigarettes.

In her bedroom I flick on the dresser lamp. She makes her bed before she goes to work, for god's sake. I finish off the apple and put the core in the ashtray on the night-table. On her cerise coverlet is a black bra and a pair of silvery silk stockings, stockings that break your heart. I put my glasses on the night-table, lie down and pull down my zipper. I probably shouldn't beat off before seeing Margot because it increases the chance that I'll go impotent but if I don't there's the premature ejaculation to consider. Either I can't get it up or I come too soon. I didn't get laid until last summer in London so I'm a little late to the party. Margot says she doesn't care. C'mon, she's lying. Nobody is *that* understanding. Nor should she settle for me. She needs some normal guy.

I feel a sweet unencumbered rising in my dick. O totem, cyclopean lighthouse, lifetime member, stand up and show uncle Mel how big you are. It doesn't take long. When I come I think of...*Charlotte*. I toss my soggy handkerchief on the floor. *Goin' out tonight?...Yeah, I got a date with Mary Fist and her five sisters.* I pry my shoes off, then my socks, and pat my wet feet on the coverlet. Maybe I'll drive into Ipswich center and pick up a typewriter ribbon. Montessori for the kids, occasional light verse for The New Yorker, harmless affairs on my book tours...

I was born in the Bronx, and raised in a small Connecticut town on Long Island Sound, right between Bridgeport and New Haven. Why my parents, both born in Poland, left the Bronx ghetto where everyone they knew (and didn't know) was Jewish and moved to a small hick town where hardly *anyone* was Jewish is a real stumper. Trying to answer that question just makes me realize that there is only so much you can know about anyone, even if they're your parents. Especially if they're your parents. And no one will fully understand *me*. Especially my children.

I got to sleep late last night and Richie roused me early so I find I'm tired. I fall asleep for a few hours. When I wake up it's 5:15 and I'm cold. I listen to the snow flick against the window. When I pull up the shade it's dark already. 5:15 and it's dark. I don't turn on any lights. I don't want to tip the balance of nature. If I need a light God will provide one. In the bathroom I crash into her scale. I take my leak on the porcelain of the bowl. No noise that way. Can't have guests hear you going number one. I fumble around the medicine cabinet for some toothpaste until I find a big tube. One thing about living alone, the toothpaste goes a lot further. Margot buys a new toothbrush every six months. The old ones she uses to clean ashtrays and typewriter keys. She cuts KitchenTips out of the newspaper. She's a good cook but she tries too hard. Peach halves on the pork chops. That kind of thing. And this butter knife. *What's wrong with* my *knife?... Nothing. Oh I don't care. Use what you want...You want me to use the fucking butter knife, I'll use it...*

Instead of working up any kind of lather I'm just spreading a swamp around in my mouth. I switch on the light and I've gone and brushed my teeth with Margot's vaginal jelly. Stupid not to have put the light on. That's what lights are for. I find the toothpaste right on the sink and clean my mouth out. A dab of Bio-Clear between the eyebrows. There's her Lady Norelco and there's her diaphragm, asleep in the little box like a gem, powdered and pampered. Before closing the cabinet I beautify my nails with her emery board.

In the living room I turn on the bottom bough of the

tree-lamp and walk over to the window. The snow is thick on the sill and I can see the Theater de Lys. The marquee lights are on already. *The Threepenny Opera*.

I hear her key. Did I flush the toilet? The apple core is still in the ashtray. Where's my handkerchief? She has snow in her hair. There's her brown cylindrical purse that looks like a pumpernickel bread. She sets her shopping bag down, unbuttons her coat, smiling at me but not saying anything. She takes off her snow-boots, then her gloves finger by finger, flips them on the table and I walk over to her. She smells from outside. Her long arms around my neck. So tall in her heels. Her mouth is cold and a little chapped. My arms around her inside the coat.

"Oh, Mel."

"Hi."

"Two months?"

"I know, it's stupid."

"What's the matter with us?"

"I don't know."

I really don't. We hold each other for a long time. When we separate and she starts taking off her coat I know something has ended and something else has begun. We may never know a finer moment and it's gone already.

"Been here long?"

"Couple hours."

"How did you amuse yourself?"

I jerked off and went to sleep.

"I read a little."

She flings her coat on the arm of the couch and starts dismantling the shopping bag. She takes out a package in white butcher paper and holds it over her head.

"Porterhouse," she says.

"Eighty-nine cents a pound."

"How did you know?"

"I saw the ad in the window walking over here. 'Weekend Beef Bonanza.'"

"I also got a surprise for dessert."

"Red Vines?"

"Oh, much better than that...Relax and I'll get you something to drink."

"I can't relax and I finished off the scotch."

She takes a bottle out of the bag and shows it to me. Johnny Walker Black Label. She sees I'm impressed and that makes her happy. I wonder if she's made it with anyone in the last couple of months. Our kids would be tall, dark-haired, intelligent, the product of a broken home.

"Oh, and there's a pack of Luckies in my purse."

I sit on the couch listening to her prepare supper and smoke a deep and meaningful cigarette. The frozen vegetables ping into a pot and she runs water over them. She pours the scotch and brings a glass out to me. Two fingers, no ice. After we click glasses and knock them down she goes back to the kitchen. Something pornographic about Margot making supper in her heels. Her big shadow stretches out of the kitchen onto the living room floor.

"How's work?"

"I got a raise, so that's good."

"Yeah."

"Yeah. How's Alex getting along?"

"So-so."

"Did he ever finish that article he was writing."

"It's a proof. No, he's still at it."

"Gee, it's been months."

"Longer than that. He's calling it *The Drama of the Space-Time Continuum*."

"Sounds like one of yours."

"I helped him with it. The "Drama" part."

"Is he still seeing Jane?"

"As little as he can."

"Meaning...?"

"Meaning sex but no relationship. He's got to get away from his Matrix once in a while. That's where Jane comes in. Jane wants more. Alex doesn't. They'll figure it out."

Margot is soaking the dishes. I put on one of her records—The Andre Previn Trio plays My Fair Lady—and I'm back on the couch. The steaks were big fuckers and the surprise was napoleons, power and greed oozing maniacally out of the sides when you bite into them. Margot finally walks in from the kitchen with her drink and sits next to me. I swing her legs on my lap, take her shoes off and warm her feet with my hands, her stockings glinting in the light. Her fingernails are short because they make her do a lot of typing. Her long fingers need long fingernails. I keep telling her that a "media executive" shouldn't have to type. She says some typing is necessary and she's not going to the mat on that issue. The phone rings. Margot says it's for me. Richie.

"Yeah."

"The last three hours have been decisive."

"I'm hanging up."

"It would be tantamount to hanging up on the twentieth century."

"The farmers and the slaves see the trumpets."

"A significant event occurred this afternoon but let me lead into that by telling you about the party tonight. Some early birds have already arrived. So rude. Anyway, Ruthie's setting up the food table as we speak and this should make the Halloween party look like a cheez-whiz Sunday brunch in Passaic.

"You understand that you're invading my privacy."

"The Interplayers and Harriet DuMont are coming over *with* that folk group I might have mentioned to you, Red Menace and the Security Risks. Lorraine Lee, nee Levinson, fresh from a three-week bomb at Slim's Pump Room, Dottie Palmer, who I've been trying to introduce you to and when I do you'll be indebted to me forever..."

"That's a sick thought."

"...Henry Werner, whose wife you know, Arthur and Lulu Goldman..."

"Do you seriously regard these people as inducements?"

"I'm just getting around to the main event."

"The Pope?"

"Even better. Are you ready?"

"I'm ready to hang up."

"Wilson Getz."

"Oh, bullshit."

"Me and Tony Silver met him at the Gold Rail this afternoon. He's in town to stage *Major Barbara*."

"Wilson Getz is coming to your party?"

"Aha. You're *impressed* with Wilson Getz."

"Compared to Harriet DuMont, yes."

"You'll like him. He goes by 'Bill.' Just plain Bill. See? He's a people guy."

"I won't like him."

"How do you know?"

"Because I won't be there."

"You don't understand. You've got to be there."

"Why, for god's sake?"

"For a lot of reasons. You know these guys. Before the first drink they're hitting you with Eisenstein's sense of anomie. I can't go through that alone. I want to create an ingratiating milieu. Remember Luther Falk and that Ibsen thing you had with him? It made him very happy. It made everyone *very happy*."

"Except me."

"Getz will be impressed if he thinks I've attracted a few intelligent types."

"Bah."

"If I could get him alone I wouldn't need you so bad. I wanted to meet him at the West End but when Silver mentioned the party, Getz said he'd love to drop by and have a drink with everyone. See? He wants an idea of what kind of people are involved. You understand the fix I'm in. Norman and Alex I have to hide."

"What makes you think he's interested at all?"

"He *said* he was. I ran through the script with him at the Gold Rail. He liked the ideas. Said it sounded *filmic*."

"So he didn't read any of it."

"I didn't have it *with* me."

"Oh, man."

"Mel, I'm asking you for a favor. I don't ask for much."

"I can't see where I'll help any. And this party. I don't want to go to any of your grotesque parties."

Margot, who started doing the dishes, pops out of the kitchen, wiping her hands with a towel.

"Party?"

"At 454. Richie wants me to meet this direct—"

Richie screaming through the receiver.

"You won't have to be there till midnight. Getz is going to the play Silver is in so you've got a few hours. Mel, there's so much at *stake*."

"All right. Shut up. I'll be there at midnight."

"Believe me when I say I'm grateful."

"Up yours."

"See you there and thanks again, Mel."

"Yeah yeah."

Margot thinks it sounds like fun.

"Give Richie his due," she says. "He throws great parties."

"This director will be there around midnight. Richie wants him to direct *The Vandals*."

"And Richie wants you to charm the hell out of him."

"Something like that. You up for it?"

"Are you kidding? After five days at Bender & Fry?"

I hear her stockings scratch at the thighs as she walks back to the kitchen. The liquefaction of her clothes.

"Leave the dishes," I say. "Let's go to bed."

I'm a glutton for punishment. She hangs the little towel on the doorknob and switches off the kitchen light. Margot has already turned on the space heater in her bedroom so it's nice and cozy. She seems happy to take off her clothes, the last vestiges of her work week. The final item is her panties. She steps out of them onto a Grecian urn. She cannot fade though thou hast not thy bliss. For the octillionth time in human history, Margot and I are about to enact the beast with two backs. Ah but first, foreplay. It must be fun having sexual intercourse. I understand both the male and female experience intense pleasure. Outside I hear drips and splats. The snow has turned into a platitudinous rain. I notice my handkerchief on the floor and surreptitiously pick it up and stuff it in my back pocket. Margot throws the blankets back and lies flat on the bed, one knee up, and looks at me as if to say, this is who I am. I take my clothes off as we look at each other, staring really. The proverb says all the world is on the tip of the tongue. Yet if I were able to spit it out wouldn't I lose everything? I decide to accept the rain completely. I crawl into bed and tell her that I'm about to transform her into an uncontrollable animal. She says, feel free. Her feet are cold. A female trait. Cold at the extremities.

As expected, I'm having a little trouble getting it up but my standard rationale is that only superficial guys never have trouble getting a hard-on. And I am many things, *many* things, but certainly not superficial. I reach over and put on the little radio, searching for that station in Paterson that we like to listen to, the radio sputtering as I turn the knob like a safecracker. I think I've got it. Close enough. A regiment of violins...*When I fall in love, it will be completely, or I'll never fall in love*...Margot's hands are messengers of lust. At the touch my body is rife with seismic flutterings. It makes me weak and dopey but if this is what they mean by sexual surrender, I'm all for it. I caress her, lick her nipples, handle her quasi-rough. I'm pretty good at this. Then she emits an abrupt, barely audible, completely understandable fart which she says is actually an expulsion of air from her vagina.

I don't know about that.

"I wouldn't care either way," she says. "I'm not a puritan."

"It was a fart."

"It was *not*."

"How can you be so sure?"

"How can I be sure? *It's my body*."

"But both orifices are only inches apart."

"This is a good time to get my diaphragm."

"I'll leave you to your own devices."

Each time I wonder if she really puts it in. It's only 98% safe anyway. Maybe she'll accidentally use toothpaste instead of vaginal jelly. Maybe I don't *want* her to put it in. Oooh Mel, so incisive. There's a one-billionth inch magic swimming in my balls and if I could exorcise it I could take my father out of his grave, spread him on the air and let him filter through eternity.

Margot returns haughtily, like she's trying to balance a book on her head. Our little exchange stopped the flow a bit. The rain continues to dribble on the chin of the window. While in the bathroom, she sprayed her My Sin between her breasts in a desperate attempt to make both of us horny. It's working, too. She goes down on me. Damn pleasurable but I can't permit too much of that lest I blow my wad. I turn her over and burrow my face in her pussy. Her cunt is like a baklava, with a big strawberry clit. She pulls me up by my hair and branches out her body. She's ready (the ripeness is all), her mouth trembling. Now, coach? Yes, Dick, get in there and stay in there. The knees go way back and wide apart like the handbook says. She's great at this. She'll make some man very happy. Calculating the square root of large numbers is an effective preoccupation during the mechanistic phase of the genital embrace. It is not uncommon among adherents of karezza to sustain phallic thrusts for as long as three weeks. I'm wanted in fourteen states for excessive virility.

Ambushed by Margot's prehensile snatch I pass that point of no return. Three goes into seven with a remainder of one, drop the four and it goes four times with a remainder of two, bring up the decimal point, into twenty-eight goes nine, drop the zero, drop the bomb, ban the bomb, bomb the bomb, unleash Chiang...When I start rolling off she says, "Stay on top of me."

Okay, fucking isn't my strong suit. I can't have everything. I should count my blessings. I haven't got a toothache. Nor have I got a sliver under my toenail. I finally roll off her and we lie there for a while, my feet warming hers, feeling like the day after my bar mitzvah, glad that it's over.

"You've lost weight," she says.

"You look great. And you've got a magnificent pussy."

"Thanks...Look, you're detumescing."

"He's scared shitless," I say.

"He's scared of you, not me."

Wow, she's right. I put a lot of pressure on my dick.

"I've got to pee," she says and when she goes into the bathroom I wipe myself up with her Kleenex. I'm getting cold with nothing on so I get under the covers but I don't want to stay in bed. I've had enough of this bed. That's right, I'm glad it's over and she knows it, so why should I light up a cigarette like Paul Henreid and make believe I'm waiting for it to get hard again. I dress myself quickly and smooth out the coverlet. There are no scratches on my body, no teeth-marks. When she returns I'm sitting on the edge of the bed. She's disappointed but I can't help it.

She ignores me and brushes her hair in front of the dresser mirror, defiance being to her beauty as dew is to the rose. As a peach-half is to the pork chop. In her nakedness, Margot seems disenchanted, a wood nymph stolen from a myth and brooding over her worldly captivity. She brushes wistfully, thinking of those days and nights when she gamboled through grateful forests. The only light comes from the living room. With her hands by her hair and her back to me, no one will ever see her again in this light, at this angle, and in this mastery of herself.

"Are you brushing your hair 500 times?"

"No."

"How many times?"

"No special amount."

"Why don't you come over here?"

"I'll put something on."

She throws on a robe and lies down behind me. She's found a spot on the ceiling, her arms by her side. I pick up her hand and kiss her tallow fingers.

"What's this?"

"I'm not crying," she says.

"Yes you are."

"It's all in my eyes. You're not really crying until a tear rolls down your cheek."

I ask, "What's the matter?" as if I didn't know.

"Nothing."

I wait, but not for long.

"You're pathetic. And so am I."

That's a hell of a thing, telling me I'm pathetic. I think it's probably rude. She dries her eyes so she can look straight at me and says again, "You're pathetic." This is nothing short of character assassination. She sits up and blows her nose with a Kleenex, and continues with, "I'm pathetic, too." Now she stands up and paces.

"What brought this on?"

"Everything. The holes in your shoes. Mostly your good spirits. I guess I expect you to be depressed. Instead, you walk around like an Irishman on St. Patrick's Day."

That's hitting below the belt.

"You're anesthetized from head to foot. But you keep up the patter and your little jokes. You can't support yourself, you can't write your book, you can't get out of the *rain*."

"What am I supposed to do about it?"

"Be inventive..."

You mean like a fiction writer?

"...I'm a human being," she says.

"I know."

"Don't say you know when you *don't* know. You don't treat me like a real person. I'm an idea to you, a bad idea..."

"Don't say that. Maybe you are an idea but you're a great idea, a beautiful idea."

"You only call me when you're horny. You said so yourself this morning."

"I'm fucked up. I'm afraid of sex. I won't lie to you no matter how much you want me to...Sit down on the bed."

"No. I know you're hung up about your mom and dad but you can't go through life using that as an excuse for whatever you need an excuse for."

I stretch out flat on the bed. The ceiling is full of her from the dresser lamp and the rain is still falling. I used to think that the twentieth century would be the last, that after 1999 life would either end with a voice booming "nice game, folks" and poof, or start all over again as amoebas in a pond, like in gin rummy when no one's gone out and you turn the deck over. The shadow moves slowly, her weight on the bed.

"Shit, Mel."

"I *am* pathetic."

"No, you're not."

"I'm a lousy lay."

"Just relax about it. Be kind to yourself."

I can't think of anything to say so I say nothing. After a while she says, "I hope I only hurt you a little bit. I'm sorry I mentioned your parents."

"It's okay. You're right about everything."

We lie there for a long time with our arms around each other. The rain has almost stopped. Finally, Margot sits up.

"We've still got time before the party. Let's walk over to Rienzi's and then we can take a cab uptown. I'll wear tinted stockings and be your girl."

I forgot about the party. She actually looks happy. She got a lot off her chest. I feel better, too, but I still have some stuff on my chest.

"Wouldn't it be nice," I say, "if it was October and we were in Vermont walking through the woods?"

"You forget, I'm allergic to poison oak."

Wood nymphs allergic to poison oak. What a lousy world.

Rienzi's is crowded. At the table next to us, two scrabble players are taking turns raping the language. *My* language. Controversy over Z-O-R. He's wearing an NYU blazer and looks like Robert Q. Lewis. He *knows* there is such a word. His girlfriend asks him to use it in a sentence which perks up my ear. He says he doesn't know exactly what it means but he thinks it's a crossword puzzle-type word for "mine entrance." She gives in. Sure, because giving in right there leads to minimal communication. To argue the point you'd be required to at least minimally communicate with this obvious maniac. At the table on the other side of us, two pipe smokers are playing the King's Gambit declined, answered with the Falkbeer Counter Gambit. Chess is intellectual skid row. Margot, her eyes still a little red, informs me that it's time to go.

Outside, the rain has stopped and a soft bearded breeze runs through the streets. On Sixth Avenue we find a cab and soon we're barreling up the West Side Highway, the wheels of the cab bumpy and sibilant. I'm back against the seat with my arm around Margot and the sidereal image of the bridge in the distance is full of promise, anything I want, name it. Just like New York.

"Does Richie want this director to direct his movie?"

"He won't be there."

"Richie?"

"Getz. Wilson Getz."

"How do you know?"

"This happens once a week. One day it's Getz, one day it's Ethel Longstreet, one day it's Mao Tse-Tung. That's right, Mao promised him that he'd do a cameo. When we arrive, we'll be notified that Getz called in sick and Richie will be drunk and do his imitation of Teddy SnowCrop."

"I think you're jealous."

"I am. I'm jealous of everybody."

"He's doing something…he's *trying* to do something."

She gives the driver a big tip, trying to make me look like some effete lowlife way over his head. Snow is banked up high on the curb but the sidewalk is slushy from the rain. Margot slides, laughing, and I catch her. In the elevator we analyze G. Gormley's penmanship.

Back in Milford I wanted to grow up and have hair on the back of my hand and have sex with slutty girls. I thought Gordie Wills was the finest person ever to walk the earth until one day he called me a kikey four-eyed, sheeny-faced, mockey-ass Jew bastard hebe. In Milford you went to the Drive-In on Friday nights. You missed the whole second feature trying to unhook her bra. Afterwards at Paul's hamburger stand out on the Post Road you bump into a few classmates checking out the scene. When one of them asks, "Gettin' much?" you come right back with, "no," and they all laugh out loud because they know you aren't kidding. She hands you all this shit about how she can't put out because Catholicism screwed her up. You drop her off, picking up on four Catholic eyes watching you through the venetian blinds. Before you go to sleep you walk along Fort Trumbull Beach to work off the blue balls.

We step off the elevator and, though 12B is four doors down, I can hear the party having a nervous breakdown.

Chapter Four

The smoke is so thick it leans against you. Everyone's sweating and screaming at each other. There's Art Gibbs, who used to work in a factory that made those hard rubber things under the toilet seat so the seat won't break when it hits the bowl. There's Loni Gumbiner, who had both ovaries removed when she was around ten because they had cancerous cysts on them but was told by her mother that it was her appendix that was removed and wasn't told the truth until she was 21. Oh, and recently married. There's Phil Bloom, just back from Nassau, plump, tan, wearing a beige suit and looking like a head cheese. There's Charlotte talking to Carlos, the beautician from Tegucigalpa who embraces Subud. There's Norman, at his post on the couch writing in his notebook, copying down everything he can hear. The shadows in his gaunt face order the chaos. Surely he'll be dead soon, and when he's dead, will I write a book about him? *Monody for an Extinct Spider*. Will it get good reviews? We find a vacant spot on the wall.

"Nice little get-together," she screams.

"A fool and his money are soon partying."

"I can't hear you," she screams.

"I'll take your coat," I scream back.

"Is there a safe place?"

"The closet in my room. Stay here. I'll bring you back something to drink."

I peristaltically make my way through everyone, people saying hi sweetie to me and hey man, what's happening. Gargoyle hairdos brush my cheeks. I would say that I didn't know these people were it not for the fact that I do. A two-foot high Christmas tree is set up on a card table in the corner of the living room with a few lights strung up around the room, instantly entering the pantheon of all-time half-ass homages to the holiday.

I bump into Antonio Silver talking to Shelly, her hair pulled back in a ponytail. We smile all around and say hello, unbelievably uninterested in each other. Shelly fed her Siamese cat Ritz crackers and never let it out of her infected one-room studio. One day, having had quite enough, the cat laid down and, like Enobarbus, died of a broken heart. She was too squeamish so I, feigning unsqueamishness, picked it up by the tail and walked it down to the garbage cans. She and Richie used to be an item while he was casting wink wink for Faith, his film's ingénue-type. *Faith, for god's sake, Richie, it's such a crummy name…Hey, it's symbolic. Anyway, it's* my *movie.* Shelly's wide patent-leather eyes and her flushed cheeks suggest innocence, but for a walk-on in a YMCA revue she would blow Dwight Eisenhower in Macy's window.

In the kitchen Harriet DuMont is picking tobacco off her tongue and raving. I hear her telling someone that Charlie Parker and Dizzy Gillespie are the Pound and Eliot of modern jazz. And now, having heard it, I can't unhear it. Maybe I can use it in my novel's savage portrait of supposedly hip New Yorkers. DuMont

98

bankrolls this Greenwich Village theater company called The Interplayers. She's also a drama critic for Thespus, a downtown rag devoted to bullshit. Once she told Richie that Chekhov was overrated. Certainly she ought to be flogged and shpritzed with insect repellent. Next to her is Randy, one of her protégés nudge nudge, an actor with her company who never says anything or looks you in the eye.

I notice the empty, once proud, pyrex casserole dish *on the floor*. Someone could at least have had the common human decency to get it off the floor, put it in the sink and run hot water over the crusty bottom. Before I'm able to make it to my bedroom I hear, "Melvin, you're a sometime practitioner of the literary arts…"

Not even a hello. She's in such a hurry to be a public nuisance.

"Where are all the *real* novels nowadays, the kind you can't put *down*?"

I could plead irresistible impulse. *We find the defendant not guilty of the axe bludgeoning mutilation of Harriet DuMont.*

"Oh, I'm sure you'll find *some* book to put down."

"How uncompromisingly droll, Melvin," she says in her best Bette Davis, flicking the ash from her Herbert Tareyton.

When I push open the door to my room I see that everyone's coat has been tossed on my bed. I'm used to this indignity when Richie throws his parties. But when the door opens wider the kitchen light falls on Marty and some girl who buries her face in my funky pillow and then, backhanded, throws Marty's jacket over her head.

"Would you tell her my seat-belt doesn't work."

"Wadya want?"

"Just trying to get to my closet."

"So do it and stop bothering the public."

"In *my* room I don't have to put up with your shit."

"So it's your cruddy room."

I hang up Margot's coat.

"So long, Marty. Tell Garbo I got a bomb in my luggage."

When I finally return Margot is still up against the living room wall, trying to stay out of harm's way. She looks great in her red dress and silvery stockings. I give her one of the two drinks I managed to carry back.

"Here. Get drunk."

"I had a feeling I'd never see you again."

"I was going to jump out the kitchen window but I couldn't get to it."

"I saw Alex."

"With Jane?"

"I didn't notice her."

"What about Richie?"

"Not yet."

"Let's find him."

Overheard as we push through the crowd: "Do you think I can do anything more dramatic with my wall?" The record player is stuck. I get no kick from cham-I get no kick from cham-I get no kick from cham-. Deeper and deeper, the trail back has sealed closed. In the fruity frosty cake of my generation, I am the thankless yeast. *Mel Montrose: Founder of Isism—The Early Years.*

Margot bumps into Hal, a guy she knows. Perfunctory introductions ensue. Hal looks like the kind of guy who goes out for the ice cubes. While they chat I squirm through the throng in the direction of Alex whose head is on the platter of people. But Richie leaps out of my pocket.

"Hey Yank, fuck my sister? Nylons? Cigarettes?"

"Where's Getz."

"He said he'd be here around 11:30," looking at his watch, which says 1:15. "Right now I'd rate him a solid no-show...Someday 1960 will seem like a long time ago."

"Your eyes look like fried eggs, basted with bacon fat."

Yes, Richie's smashed and just getting started.

"It's true. I'm boozing it up...I just saw Margot and may I say, at the risk of seeming indelicate, that she is an extremely attractive and well-developed young woman. Albeit a foot taller than myself."

"Are you paying all these extras?"

"I like crowds...I got a terrific idea for a movie. Robert Alda in The Mel Allen Story....or, hey, what about Mel Allen in The Robert Alda Story?...When *The Vandals* premieres I'll throw a party that will make Baby Pignatari look like a Trappist monk. Famous names will be there from all walks of life...Getz is supposedly Mister Integrity. I mean you don't think a man would go back on his word, do you, Mel?"

"Hard to imagine anyone going back on his or her word."

"I see two empty chairs so why don't we sit on them because I don't want to spill any expensive scotch when I pass out."

Richie blazes a trail, his drink held high, and I follow in his wake. We sit on uncomfortable folding chairs. He rubs the glass across his forehead.

"He told me to my face that he'd be here."

"He still might come."

"You're right. There's still a, say, point nine per cent chance he'll show up...So tell me, how's everything down at the baloney factory?"

Richie looks into the crowd the way you look into the ocean. He points at a young actress named Paula with hair down to her waist, a wide leather belt and chalky ankles.

"What do you think of Paula?"

"I don't think of Paula."

"Let me tell you something fascinating about her. She fucks."

"I'm afraid of sex."

I want to tell everyone the truth, even if everyone's too drunk to notice.

"I'll introduce you."

"Nope."

He continues to scan the crowd, then lets it all come out.

"I'm drunk and pissed and lonely and tired and fed up, really fed up, and probably more pissed than lonely but maybe more drunk than pissed. I've been holding my breath for a long time and I'm running out of oxygen. No one cares. Do you hear what I'm saying?"

As he leans over to make his point he falls off the folding chair. I help him up and brush off his pants.

"It seems I've turned into an oaf."

"It's these Mickey Mouse folding chairs."

"Did any of the guests notice?" he asks with mock propriety.

"I don't think so. They're as wasted as you are."

"Good. I'd hate to find myself a squib in Winchell's column tomorrow. It's so difficult getting to the top and so easy to fall awkwardly on your fucking face."

"How true."

He wound up spilling the scotch anyway. Now he's

getting an unfinished one behind him on the arm of the couch. There's a match in it.

"Did I tell you I'm sort of with someone tonight? She just flew in from Moline, Illinois."

"Who's that?"

"You remember Shelly's old roommate, an actress?"

"Sophie?"

"Sonia. On the other hand, she might have left. Maybe she's not entirely devoted to me. Have you noticed how sometimes a girl isn't entirely devoted?"

"That's the booze talking."

"Why did he say he was going to be here? He could have just said 'maybe' or 'I'll try' or something less definite than 'I will be there.' It's not classy. It's not *right*. You live by a code or you're a weenie."

He hiccups, then burps a long low one, staring petulantly at Paula's back. I finish off my drink with a big swallow.

"In my memoirs I'll take him apart. He'll become an object of ridicule."

"Damn right."

"Soon I'll be too busy making film history to waste my time with midgets like him. *Mr. Getz is on line three, Mr. Kovak... Tell all callers I'm in Japan for the afternoon.*"

He points in horror at my empty glass. Yeah, good idea. I need to get smashed, too.

The kitchen seems far away. This mob is indefatigable. They'll hear the will. Making my way through the darkroom I hear Harriet DuMont droning, Randy by her side like a tumor. There's Charlotte again. I wonder if I should tell her that I jerked off to her today. She's laughing, happy to be alive. In the deep recesses of Charlotte's soul it's always one o'clock in the afternoon. She's watching Marty play on his new set of drums, an early Christmas present from his father, accompanying Henry Werner on a piano Richie rented. Henry is torturing *Fur Elise*, and smiling serenely like he's Vladimir fucking Horowitz. On the upper keys, Carl Gruenfeld plays Chopsticks. His blonde bimbo-esque date says, "Oh don't, Carl, you're spoiling it." I can't find Alex anymore, but I see Antonio Silver in the corner moving in on Loni Gumbiner.

"Hey, Tony."

"Hello, Mel. Finish your novel yet?" he asks with a smirk.

"Except for a few finishing touches. Say, Tony, I heard that Wilson Getz was supposed to be here tonight."

"I guess he changed his mind."

"Hm. I'm wondering where I can reach him?"

"Why?"

"I want to speak to him. What do you mean 'why?'"

"He's a very busy man."

"Where's he staying, Silver?"

"I'm not sure I should divulge that information."

"I got your *divulge*."

"Now just a minute."

"After that minute I'm going to get violent."

"He's at the McAlpine, for heaven's sake."

"Let's face it, Silver. You're chicken."

In the kitchen I sit down and pour myself some of Richie's expensive scotch, knock it down and pour another. The door to my room is still closed and it dawns on me who Greta Garbo is. The barnacled casserole dish has been kicked under the kitchen table.

"Sonia, you're a despicable creep."

I yell again.

"Sonia, why don't you take Marty and go back to Moline fucking Illinois before you make an even greater fucking travesty of human relations."

I refill my glass. Margot comes in laughing with Hal and another couple, Milt and Edith. After some enervating introductions they all sit down with me. I'm feeling a tad anti-social at the moment but I don't want to piss off Margot. Hal seems to be entertaining her. He'd take good care of her, go out and work so she could stay home and let her nails grow. When she laughs she shows her neck, tight and white, an unscathed obelisk. Hal doesn't joke around so much now because he knows I'm her date and you're not supposed to make girls laugh in front of their date.

Everyone knows that. Edith sits there watching me like I'm a fly she's about to swat but her husband Milt seems okay, receding hairline, the kind of guy that calls girls gals, the kind of guy who steps out of the shower to piss in the toilet, the kind of guy who goes out with the guy who goes out for the ice cubes.

"Margot tells me you're a writer."

"That's right, Hal. Have I been published? No not yet haha. What sort of writing do I do? Fiction, Hal. You know, where you make it up as you go along? What's my novel about? Man's inability to give a shit."

"Oh, Mel."

"Margot's got it all wrong. I'm not being rude. I'll strike anyone who says otherwise."

Hal gets a lot of points for smiling and asking, "What's that you're drinking?"

"Scotch. Let me pour you one."

"Just a little."

"That's the spirit. Milt and Edith?"

They both lift their drinks to show they have one already. As I liberally pour Hal some of Richie's expensive scotch in a red paper cup, Margot glares at me. Yes, "glares" is the only word that will do. I look at her.

"Be a pal, Margot. I'm sick in the soul. It's a variety of religious experience."

Edith is trying to arch her eyebrow.

"Edith, did you know that if you stretched out the subway system end to end in a single line almost everyone would have to take a bus to work?"

The four of them smile politely and rise at the same time. Did they rehearse that?

"Are you leaving the party?" I ask her.

"Do you want me to?"

"No. At least don't go with Hal. That would probably hurt me for some ludicrous reason. No offense, Hal."

"I understand."

"Good. Someday you can explain it to *me*."

Margot looks at Hal, then me, and says, "I'll be inside when you're ready."

As they turn to go I say to them, "Thank you for putting up with a guy who is really pathetic."

Margot frowns. I forgot she called me that. Or I remembered. When they leave I decide to resume my communication with Sonia in person because I'm sick and tired of them ignoring me. I kick the door open like Richard Widmark in *Kiss of Death*. They're talking quietly but the light's off and I can't see much.

Marty says, "What now?"

"I want to talk to Sonia from Moline, Illinois."

He says, "This is not Sonia from Moline, Illinois. This is Marylou from Jackson Heights. Sober up, dipshit."

Damn. I get Margot's coat and return to the kitchen

just as two giggling couples walk in.

"Hey wadya say, Mel, for cryin' out loud?"

"Hey Carl Gruenfeld and his three friends."

I'm a tad out of it as we swap banalities for a few minutes. When they leave I drop Margot's coat on a chair, fix myself another drink and polish it off in one quaff because that's the kind of guy I am. The table is still laden with bottles of booze. I grab an unopened pint of Cutty Sark and put it in the pocket of Margot's coat. One more thing remains in my new-found mission to set the universe on its proper course. I take the casserole dish off the floor and put it in the sink and run hot water in it. It's a great dish. You can bake in it, use it as a server, a salad bowl, fruit bowl.

The kitchen clock says 2:15. The party is still humming. Long thin lines of laughter shoot over the din and are sucked out the open window that faces the Hudson. Hugo Phelps, the bass player with the Security Risks, is next to me talking to Carlos, the beautician from Tegucigalpa who embraces Subud. Hugo says to Carlos, "Cogito ergo sum, baby."

Margot is talking to Richie. When I catch her eye she starts to sidle through to me, Richie stumbling behind her.

"Our revels now are ended," I say.

"Richie says, "Isn't it a tad early?"

"It's either early or late. I never know."

"Feel better?" Margot asks me.

"I'm okay. Sorry I acted poorly. If they're still here I should apologize."

"They left. But they're fine. They've been with drunk, belligerent people before."

Richie says, "Sorry you have to run. There's still some scotch left."

"Save it for your New Year's Eve party."

I help Margot on with her coat. She feels the bottle in her pocket, gives me that look and extends her hand to Richie.

"Nice seeing you again," she says, extending her hand to Richie..

"Go with God, my child. Walk in his light."

"I'll try."

"...and if you ever have the need to come over to the rectory for confession and a cup of hot cider..."

I once called him Father Flanagan for taking in the misfits that live in 454. So sometimes he does the clergyman bit. A private joke between us.

"...You may kiss my ring. Unless that seems unhygienic."

Instead he bends over and kisses *her* ring that her grandmother gave her, a wide band of gold and a purple stone. Over his shoulder I see Silver has finally nailed Loni Gumbiner to the wall. Richie hiccups and burps again. Like lightning and thunder.

He says, "Shall I tell my man to bring a car around

front?"

"No need, old sport. My elephants are outside…Keep punchin', man."

"I'm going to make my movie. I don't need anyone."

"The thing is, you do."

"I don't need Getz."

"Right. Fuck him."

"*Fuck* him. You hit it right on the head."

"I'm glad you see it that way."

"Still, the prick could've called."

"We all could've done a lot but we didn't and we won't. Do it yourself and you won't have to thank anyone. Except on Oscar night."

"I'll still have you to thank."

"For what?"

"For coming tonight."

"You're drunk."

"I would've felt worse if Getz came and you didn't."

"Now you're jiving."

"But I'm not," he says with that look, non-smiling, staring at me, body frozen in arms-up mode that makes me believe him and believe *in* him.

He waves to us and tips to the side. Or was that me? The door closes and I stare at it. 12B and a small peekaboo window for undesirables. *Kovak? Yes, he used to live here but he moved to Venezuela.* Margot turns me around and walks me to the elevator. The hall floor is like bathroom tile, octagonal chicken wire. She presses for the elevator and I disengage from her and lean against the wall. I can hardly stand up. She stares at me. I wonder if she ever thinks of her grandmother and how she's wearing her ring from so long ago. She stares and stares. It's hard to stare at someone. You've got to keep switching from eye to eye. *It's impossible to stare into both eyes at once.* She leans in, arms by her side, tilting her head, closing her eyes, kissing me so tender I can feel four lips. I make a move for the elevator when the doors open but she keeps me right there against the wall with just her torso, no arms or hands. The doors close and the elevator whooshes down without us.

Chapter Five

We're heading toward Broadway for a cab but Margot spots one on the Drive. She tells him Bedford but he thinks it's in Brooklyn. No, I pipe in, that's where Duke Snider's home runs used to wind up.

"Bedford *Street*. Yeah. In the Village, right?"

"Right."

"I live in Brooklyn so that's the first thing I thought of."

He says he was pissed when the Dodgers moved west. He'll have to take a number. One morning the rulers of the universe decided to take away my Giants *and* the Dodgers and make it impossible to see Willie Mays play baseball.

"Those teams are just in it for the buck...Yeah, it's a business like anything else...you go where the money is."

"Margot, this guy is a cynic."

He's back in Ebbets Field. Schaefer beer in the bleachers. I hit him with Eddie Miksis and Gene Hermanski and he comes right back with Erv Palica and Vic Lombardi. Because the Dodgers and Giants have only been gone for two years, the wounds are still there, like the rubble in East Berlin after the war. My Giants are in San Francisco and I'm here. There it is in a nutshell. I take the Cutty Sark out of Margot's coat pocket and rip the plastic off. Plastic rips nice.

He drives toward the West Side Highway. The lean-to sky is splotched with clouds melting, all the stars turned on and a big moon with a ring around it, indicating that it either will or won't rain tomorrow. Stalagmites go down, stalactites come up. Thank god I had at least two years of college. Now I can not only predict the weather and know my way around caves but I also learned, for example, that the Pre-Raphaelites didn't live before Raphael, as some incredibly ignorant people might suppose.

"Cabs give one a false sense of importance," I say to all who can hear.

"I asked Richie about that director. He said the guy couldn't make it because he was suddenly called to Japan. What's that all about?"

"Want some?"

"No. Why didn't that guy show up?"

"I don't know."

"Didn't he call or anything?"

"Nope."

"How inconsiderate."

"Just a little snort?"

"*No.*"

Early one morning, just when it was getting light, Richie was on 42nd Street walking to the Grand Central subway station on his way home to 454. It was quiet and drizzly and when he looked up a few stories at the Commodore Hotel he saw a woman's arm reach out to see if it was raining. All he saw was an arm through the drapes and then it was gone. I remember he said that when she pulled her arm back in she took the morning with her.

"Did he feel bad about being stood up?"

"You heard him. 'Fuck Wilson Getz.'"

"That's what he said but-"

"Dammit, why don't you have a drink?"

"Richie deserves better."

It's like swallowing a handful of needles. I take another swig and another, gritting my teeth like a maniac. Richie deserves better.

"Sitting there with him on those folding chairs, all of a sudden I felt how he felt. You just can't depend on anyone in this life. They ain't gonna come through for you."

Margot looks at me like she's going to say something. Instead she rests her head on my shoulder which is nice but her hair tickles my face. I spend a few furtive seconds trying to brush it away but there's always one or two annoying strands tickling my face. You'd think I'd be spared these tiny aggravations. The cab moves up the ramp onto the highway, up where the river and the night bullshit you along, where vows are cheap as borscht. Over Margot's head I stare at the cruel lie of the skyline, the apartment lights like IBM cards, where the city flexes its muscles and hides its heel in the morning we'll all wake to.

"You wanna hear a joke?"

"Okay," she says with mock enthusiasm.

"Pretend I'm a bus driver and you ask if the crosstown busses run all night."

"Do the crosstown buses run all night?"

"No. You've got to say, 'Crosstown buses run all night?'"

"Okay. Crosstown buses run all night?"

"Doodah, doodah."

I think my cortex was passed during my last bowel movement. I also think I'm spinning and probably nauseous.

"You're so leggy and yummy. It's frightening. Every time you spread your legs the earth rumbles."

"Do you want to make love?"

"You always have to turn it into something dirty."

"I didn't mean right here."

"Look at yourself. You're a fucking amazon."

"You're saying I'm a freak?"

"I haven't got a small penis, have I? It's at least average, isn't it?"

"Shh, he can hear you."

"Did you know that Harriet DuMont once slept with Wilhelm Reich? You'd think she couldn't be all bad, but it turns out she is."

As we approach the 19th Street exit I realize that

116

whoever is responsible for this evening has not only eliminated Rosencrantz and Guildenstern *and* the gravedigger's scene but is also about to get rid of Fortinbras. Fortinbras, however, is indispensable. He restores order.

"Take the next left. 19th Street exit."

"You ain't going to Bedford Street?"

"No. This left. Just stay in this lane."

Margot looks at me funny, says, "Where are we going?"

"Restaurant."

"I've got food at my place."

"Out of the question."

"Where to, Miss?"

Why is he asking *her* all of a sudden?

I answer, "2nd Avenue and 10th Street. And step on it," then whisper in Margot's ear, "I always wanted to say that."

"You're the boss," he says.

"Why do you want to go to a-"

"Because I'm the boss, okay?"

"Okay. You know you're very drunk, though."

"Of course I know."

"All right."

"Margot?"

"What?"

"The shadows are sculpting your beautiful face."

"Are they?"

"Sometimes I think of us getting married and having a baby together."

"Please don't."

"Makepeace. If it's a boy. Makepeace Montrose. Two alliterative trochees. Nifty, huh?."

She looks at me and shakes her head back and forth. Not in a good way. Glug glug glug. I screw the top back on the Cutty Sark and lay it on the seat. I'm sober enough to know I'm drunk enough. We've arrived. Margot gives the cabbie another big tip. Okay I'm an absolute bum. Point taken. Can we change the subject? I leave the half-filled bottle on the back seat.

Out on the sidewalk I think of straightening my tie but I'm not wearing one. Inside, my glasses steam up. There's an old woman with a bowl of soup at one of the tables along the wall and an old man in back reading the newspaper. The odors conspire here. I think of Sunday mornings. *You get dressed while I warm up the car. We can be back before Mama wakes up.* Driving to Fox's deli in New Haven and then the bakery for challah and Kaiser rolls.

A young guy with glasses pops up from behind the counter. In a few years he'll take over the business and have a son who'll take over the business and he'll have a son who'll take over the business…There it all is, the familiar briskets and herrings and salamis and smoked whitefish and a butte of chopped liver. Laid out in front of him is the massive vermillion lox. Your father has expired.

"He wants your order," Margot says to me.

"First, what are *you* going to have?"

"I can't eat. Just coffee."

"Okay, you can have some of mine."

You knew the bumbas were ready when they split open from the boiling. They were too fat for the hot dog bun and you ate them with the special mustard you got from Alpert, the sycophantic butcher. Leviticus expressly forbids sexual relations with hooved animals.

Margot says, "Why don't we sit down at a table?"

He stares at me vapidly with his arms folded.

"I would like a bumba."

"Pardon?"

"I would like a bumba. To start off with."

"What's a bumba?"

What kind of crack is that?

"Would you rephrase that question?"

"What is a bumba?"

"Hm, that's very close to the way you phrased it before. Are you looking for a fat lip?"

"Mel, don't. Please don't. Let's sit at a table."

"I can handle this. Where's your boss?"

"He's not here."

"Where is he?"

"He's home. *Sleeping.*"

"Could you call him up?"

"Are you crazy?"

"Don't walk away from me, you charlatan."

Margot is pulling my goddam arm. I won't have my arm pulled. She tells me I'm yelling. I happen to know I'm not yelling. She's actually apologizing to this guy as though I'm some kind of public nuisance.

"Can't you just order something else? He doesn't have what you want."

"He has it, Margot. Don't be naïve."

Now he walks back.

"Listen, mister. I'll be glad to take your order. Just don't give me a hard time."

"I'll have a ham sandwich."

"Drunken bastard."

"I'll rip your foreskin off."

Margot leads me to a table in the far corner. Maybe it's best she intervene lest we have one deceased deli clerk on our hands.

"Impudent prick."

"You have this violent streak."

"You're right. I gotta make sure I beat his head into a plowshare."

"It frightens me."

I was always angry at myself for being non-violent. I would've been so good at violence. A bunch of kids used to chase me home from school. They said I killed Christ. They called me names—kike, sheenie, hebe, the usual, and the one that hurt the most, the ultimate epithet: *Jew*. When I got older and bigger I could defend myself but I couldn't bring myself to hit anyone. One day this kid, Cameron Dunn, called me a kike and I jumped him and got him down on the ground and starting punching him—*on his thigh*. Yeah on the side of the thigh where it doesn't hurt at all. The only thing I hurt was my hand. After a while Cameron, on the ground with me on top of him, looked up at me—and smiled.

My father told me this story: He was about 14-15, living in a small town in Poland when a bunch of German soldiers passed through. Poland was a battlefield between German and Russian soldiers, with Poland doing most of the suffering. These German soldiers had a kid with them, a kind of mascot, also in uniform, also about my father's age. He came up to my father and started making fun of him, calling him names, entertaining the older soldiers. Then he punched my father right in the mouth. My dad went down on the ground while the soldiers laughed along with the kid who stood over him. My father knew that if he fought back he would have been shot. So he just stayed there on the ground. The kid gave him one final kick in the ribs and they all moved on.

Maybe that's why I didn't bash in Cameron Dunn's face.

A waitress approaches our table with menus, looking at me askance. She's all made up, like the Israeli soccer team was going to walk in any minute.

"Do you want something to eat?" Margot asks.

"Nah. Just coffee."

"Two coffees," she says, and the waitress picks the menus back up and leaves, still eyeing me.

The old guy in back gets up, folds the paper under his arm and pushes his chair back under the table. The walls are light blue turning lavender where they meet the mint green ceiling. Fat yellow columns with empty coat-hangers like spiders. Wooden Corinthian capitals. Used to be we'd walk into Fox's and feel indestructible. You can't do a Jewish play on an empty stage. We Jews don't live at Grover's Corners.

"My father died in Miami on New Year's Eve. Did I ever tell you that?"

"Yes."

"Now *that's* what I call dying. Miami is pretty weird but we still had a good time. I remember us walking into a bar on Collins Avenue and having a drink together. That was the single most exciting moment in my life. I never met one guy, I know there must've been guys, but I never met one guy who ever had a drink with his father in a bar…In the morning he said he felt bad, so we canned the trip to Havana. In the afternoon he felt worse so I drove him to Mercy Hospital. He went into a coma right away and died late that night, just before sunrise. It was actually New Year's Day. A New Year. A new era. New everything. Dad was 56. I was 21, and I was supposed to be a man…Nothing half-ass about my father. That guy knew how to die. It must be a special talent you cultivate your whole life. I'd like to die with as much style. Maybe during my son's graduation or on his wedding day."

"Why make yourself miserable?"

The formica table-top is full of boomerangs, every which way. I look up at Margot. Her nose is slightly crooked. Everyone's is, I understand.

"Give me a dime. I need to make a phone call."

"Sure but it's late."

"Give me a dime, pretty please."

"Okay."

There's a booth in back. The phone book weighs a ton. I keep my finger pressed down on the number. I dial and there's the ring.

Lance Blatt, eat your heart out.

"Good morning, the McAlpine."

"Wilson Getz, please. I forgot his room number."

"Is he expecting your call? It's rather late and we wouldn't want to disturb him."

"Didn't he leave you a note to expect my call?"

"Let me check his box."

He's checking his box.

"His box is empty."

"Oh gee. Bill would forget his head if it weren't attached to his shoulders. Look, he'll be in a helluva fix if he doesn't hear from me, so if you'd just ring his room you'll be doing him a big favor."

"Of course. One moment, please."

Two rings, three rings, four rings, five rings.

"Hello."

"Wilson Getz?"

"Yes. Who is this?"

"Mel Montrose. M-O-N-T-R-O-S-E."

"What can I do for you?"

"You had an appointment with Richie Kovak and you didn't keep it. Nor did you call him to explain. As a result he was waiting all night for you. Why did you do that?"

"Is this a prank or something?"

"What were you, *born* a big shot? If you don't want to help, why bullshit someone? Who the fuck are *you*."

"Who are *you*? A friend of his?"

"Listen to me, Getz. You're a blowhard and a bum."

"If you call back, I'll have the police trace your number."

"Wait, I want to tell--"

He didn't give me a chance. He didn't give me the slightest opportunity to explain my position. Coffins out of old phone booths. It's so hot and I'm so tired...Tell me, what's the undiscovered country like? Can you hear me? If I talk low, can you hear me? Everyone's gone now. You look good. Just like you're lying in bed, oversleeping. Of course, I never saw you oversleep. You were always the first one up, huh? Say something. Through the phone. I've got the phone pressed to my ear. Say anything, anything that pops into your head. Whisper...please...

"Mel?"

"What?"

"You were sleeping. Put the phone back on the hook. That's it. Come, I'll help you up. We'll go home now."

"Home?"

"Yes."

"Really?"

"Yes."

Margot paying the check. The coat-hanger spiders. Spiders aren't insects like a lot of outrageously ignorant people think. They're arachnids. So there and haha on everybody. College gave me something to fall back on. I'd rather have something to fall *forward* on. Like Anita Ekberg. Steam on the inside of the door. Out on the sidewalk. He wasn't there. He certainly wasn't on the phone. He would've said so.

"Margot, this cabdriver looks like Wendell Corey."

"Does he? Here, you get in first."

"Did anyone ever tell you you look like Wendell Corey?"

"Huh?"

"Bedford Street, please," Margot says.

"Yes, ma'am"

She guides me up the stairs. This Margot, she is fucking A all right.

"I'm tellin' ya, they broke the mold when they made you."

"Did they?"

"You're taking care of me, aren't you?"

"Yep...Just a few more steps."

"I have caused you, uh, let me count the ways, sadness annoyance, embarrassment, ennui...what else? There are more ways but I can't think of any right at the moment"

"Well, don't bother your pretty head."

"Pathetic isn't even the word for it. I mean every

time up I ground out weakly to second base. I'm a parasite and a quisling. Still, sometimes I come up with a good one. Like my old man used to say, even a stopped clock is right twice a day. Crosstown buses run all night?"

"Doodah, doodah."

Ha ha. Margot cracks me up. She catches me on the last step. Glad it's only one flight. She kinda leans me against the wall while she gets the key from her purse. I see no reason to dawdle in the living room so I roll into the bedroom and lie on my favorite coverlet while Margot takes off my shoes. She makes a rude remark about the cardboard, says she wants to buy me shoes. I couldn't let her. A man's gotta buy his own shoes. Unless he's broke. My first ever girlfriend was Virginia Baldwin in the sixth grade. We used to write notes to each other in class. On my first ever date we went to the movies to see *Good News*, a college musical with June Allyson, Peter Lawford, Mel Torme, somebody else, but we didn't walk in together. We just met at the candy counter. Either I didn't want to pay for her ticket or couldn't. Can't remember. She wore a white silky blouse that gave me a little shock whenever I touched it, which was often. I made jokes about it. See, that's how I've always dealt with stuff like that. After the movie I walked her home all the way down Gulf Street and when we got to her front door I kissed her. My first ever kiss. That summer she moved to Ohio and I never saw her again. She sent me a valentine the next February and kept sending valentines each year until I was in high school.

Saturday, December 17, 1960

Chapter Six

Margot is up and about. She stalks the bed, making just enough noise to see if I respond. Ha. She doesn't know who she's dealing with. Feigning sleep is one of my specialties.

"You awake?...It's beautiful out..."

"nnn."

I'm so good at this that it seems unfair.

"Coffee's ready when you are," she says on the way back to the kitchen.

I absolutely refuse to describe the sun shining through the venetian blinds, except perhaps to remark in passing that the day rides down the valley on a golden horse.

I recall raising my voice last night. But I didn't count on dealing with that imposter at the deli.

Margot returns, sees I'm awake and says, "I've got a great idea. Let's go skating at Rockefeller Center."

She crashes on the bed and starts reminiscing about the last time she went skating.

"C'mon, I'll make you a nice breakfast."

"Do you have Bromo-Seltzer?"

"Hung over?"

"Actually, I'm not. I just feel I had a better time the night before if I take some Bromo-Seltzer the next morning."

"Of course you do. I'll see what I have."

My glasses on the night-table. Noon exactly, according to her Westclox Electric. She must have taken my clothes off. They're all hanging neatly over a chair. I wonder if she exploited my vulnerability. I know. I'll check my hymen, see if it's intact. I'm out of bed buttoning my shirt when she returns with the stuff, crinkly and sputtering.

"This is Alka-Seltzer."

"That's right."

"You haven't got Bromo-Seltzer?"

"Now you' going to tell me there's a difference."

"I *was* going to, yes, but I see you have a closed mind on the subject."

It seems obvious that the smaller crystals would dissipate faster and more homogeneously than a fat clumsy tablet. *The Intelligent Woman's Guide to Carbonation.*

"Margot, about last night..."

"What?"

"You're going to think I'm crazy."

"I already think you're crazy."

"I see you took my clothes off. You didn't...take advantage...I mean..."

"Oh."

"You didn't, did you?"

131

"I'm afraid I did."

"So it's true."

"Finish it."

"That's enough."

"It won't work if you don't finish it."

"It's terrible."

"Finish it."

She pinned her hair back with one of those Macdougal Street tortoise-shell barrettes. She's wearing black leotards, a herringbone wrap-around skirt and a sweater the color of baby shit. I feel pretty good. Something about last night. I got off my ass and I stood up for something. Corny but...and not only that but I don't have a toothache. She walks by me to the kitchen with promises of breakfast, swinging her herringbone ass and peeking vamp-style over her shoulder. Playful this morning. Unlike the usual gothic Margot. Even that tan sweater is a pleasant change from dun, ash or umber, depending on her mood.

I've got my pants on and this is the third straight day for these socks. Fourth maybe. And I definitely need new cardboard. She's making the bed, telling me about seeing Tosca last week and bumping into Cindy Golden during intermission.

"She looked great."

Cindy Golden has always looked great, and always *will* look great. She's got the "great" thing down.

Breakfast appears on the kitchen table, which is covered with a cheerful red-and-white checkered tablecloth.

"Isn't skating expensive? Renting skates and all that? Maybe we shouldn't."

"Really, it's too dreary talking about it. I have money."

"Okay."

Not exactly a fight to the finish.

"Should I put more toast up?"

"No, thanks,"

"Is it the way you like it?"

"You mean gently ambered with just the suggestion of rigidity? Yes. Terrific."

"I'm so proud of myself."

"Don't get complacent."

"Don't worry, I know better. How are the eggs?"

"First-rate. Near-perfection."

"Near?"

"Excellent. Also terrific."

"But flawed."

"Everything has a flaw. The Parthenon has a flaw. Indeed, the very idea of flawlessness is flawed."

"Where did I goof?"

"Stop it."

"I want to know."

"Why?"

"So I can be flawless next time."

"Okay, the bubbles and the crackle on the perimeter indicate a non-optimum flame. Also, the whites were--"

"Actually, I'm sorry I brought it up."

"Perfectly all right."

My mother called a fried egg a bullseye. She cooked it hard on both sides in a little concave pan. We like to think we chew up and down but we don't. We chew in a rotary motion. Oooh Mel.

"I never got to speak to Alex and Jane last night," Margot says. "Did you?"

"No. I think they stayed in his room most of the time. He does that sometimes."

"I'm glad we fought last night," Margot says.

"Are you?"

"Sometimes I get so mad at you and say nothing. And you know why?"

"Yes."

"Because the satisfaction I get from expressing my anger isn't as great as the satisfaction I get from saying nothing and resenting you for making me angry."

"Man, you are complex."

"Resentment is always negotiable. You know?"

"Yes."

"I can carry it around with me for as long as I want and I can cash it in whenever I choose."

"You little devil."

"From now on I'm going to tell you what a bastard you are."

We eat our bacon and eggs and toast in silence. Very enjoyable. I remember reading that Thomas Carlyle and Ralph Waldo Emerson were hanging out at Carlyle's place, sitting in front of the fireplace and not saying a single word all night. When Emerson finally left, Carlyle told him how much he enjoyed his company.

"Funny that the tongue is always in a state of suspension. It's like going through life with your arm raised. The tongue just hangs around in the middle of your mouth. It never leans or lies on anything. You would think it lies on the bottom of your mouth, wouldn't you?"

"Yes, I would, Mel."

"But it doesn't. It's suspended all the time and, like a well-trained German Shepherd, is ready to perform whatever task becomes necessary, especially the task of exploring the mid-region of your naked, or even clothed, body."

"Last night you said I was leggy and yummy."

"You still are."

"Think so?"

"Yes, you coquette."

"Are you going to do anything about it?"

"You mean like have my way with you?"

"Exactly."

The telephone, that great deus ex machina, rings in the living room. Margot pushes away from the table with her eyes still looking into mine. So sexy.

"Let me get it," I tell her. "Finish your breakfast."

It's probably Richie with some post-game highlights.

"Whitey Lockman speaking."

"I'm calling AL 6-3655."

"Yes, can I help you?"

"If Margot is there I'd like to speak to her."

"Soitenly."

This is the date she forgot about. Dinner at P.J. Clarke's, tickets for some terrible musical, then cocktails at the Hickory House. His cufflinks flash in the candlelight. His socks go half way up his calf. And he's a great fuck.

"For you."

She left a little bacon on her plate. I pop it in my mouth.

"Hello...Oh, hi Jerry..."

Jerry, is it? He's filthy rich. Uses words like irrespective, necessitate, exemplify. In terms of."

"...yes, of course...haha..."

Probably a great dancer.

"...so-so, and yourself?..."

Bats left, throws right..

"...oh, he's an old friend...gee, I'm not...no...I'm not sure..."

It's official. I'm eavesdropping.

"...that would be better...yes...I can't promise but I think so...fine...bye..."

She returns and sits back down with no comment. Finally: "What happened to my last piece of bacon?"

"Beats me."

"No one leave the room," she says, biting into her toast.

"You could've gone out if you wanted to."

"I know," she says casually, and sips her coffee.

"I mean you might have preferred a night on the town, if you'll forgive that particular locution."

"Jerry is an unemployed sculptor."

"Really?"

She shoots me a patronizing smile and shakes her head. I get up to hit the bathroom where I throw water on my face and, in case we do wind up back in bed, brush my teeth with her Crest (with my finger). On the toilet I'm having a splendid bowel movement, reading the back of the Phisohex bottle. If I continue at 454 much longer I'll wind up in a solarium somewhere, making lanyards and eating Gerber's strained plums. But if I became in care of Margot Jurgenson I see similar atrophy and obsolescence. Obviously, she deserves better. The phone again. Margot says it's Richie.

"Luke Easter speaking."

"Getz just called me."

"Getz?"

"Your phone call to him ruined me."

"He told you I called?"

"Of course. God, you even had to spell your name."

"I don't get it."

"He showed up last night right after you left."

"You saw him *last night*?"

"That's what I'm saying. He didn't stay long. He said he was tired but wanted to stop by and say hello."

"Oh shit."

"Are you aware of the significance of your call?"

"I was drunk."

"That's your *excuse*?"

"How was I to know he'd finally show up?"

"You might have waited to find out."

"Oh fuck, I'm sorry."

"Now he thinks we're a bunch of ham 'n' eggers. Your phone call destroyed an embryonic business relationship and a lot of interest in *The Vandals*."

"What are the chances of patching things up?"

"I'll say none because I think we can rule out slim."

"I could call him up and apologize."

"Save it."

"I'm really sorry. Damn."

"He told me I personally shouldn't be blamed for one rotten apple in my organization blah blah blah but he was obviously throwing me a bone. He's real eccentric. He frowns on being verbally assaulted in the middle of the night. *He thinks it's rude.*"

"I don't know what to say."

"Getz is a big potato. He doesn't want to fuck around."

"I just wanted to get in a few licks for you."

"I've become pretty good at getting in my own licks and I don't need help from an up-and-coming cynic who donates an occasional evening to fend off the philistines. I've been trying for almost two years to get a break like last night."

"I know it's been a rough road."

"Rough? I'm on my ninth life."

"I couldn't feel worse than I do."

"That's all I have to say. Anyway, someone's waiting for the booth."

"Where are you?"

"The Gold Rail, reconnoitering. Maybe I'll start a little business. Make educational toys or something."

"I'll see you later," I say, but he already hung up.

Margot's been listening, leaning out of the kitchen with the dish towel in one hand, rubbing circles on a plate.

"That man arrived after we left the party? Getz?"

"It's all so unspeakable."

"Is that who you called last night from the deli?"

"Let's get out of here."

I cut out some new cardboard from the flap of one of Margot's boxes and fit them in my shoes, trimming them with her scissors. I'm trying to relive last night, what I said, what Getz said. Boy, did I fuck up. Margot is waiting, holding my overcoat open for me. My arm gets caught in the ripped lining and while I straighten it out I smell the coat's armpit odor, a miasma from the core of this rotten apple.

Chapter Seven

It's cold but the sun is out and the wind is twisting and leaping across the open space of Sheridan Square. The melting snow makes a steady dribble from the eaves and the awnings and the fire escapes, but the sky is clear, mostly blue with just a few wispy clouds like the veins in marble.

Margot's tufted jacket has a fat white fur collar. She picks up a Times and we walk down the subway entrance and through the turnstiles. She seems to know two females waiting on the platform. Our train arrives and they enter a different car which is good because I'm not in the mood to meet anyone. We sit across from an old lady wearing a Persian lamb coat, the single goal and single achievement of all four of my aunts.

"I never knew you could skate," I tell Margot.

"I love skating. Gee, I never thought...Can you skate?"

"With a set of parallel bars, probably."

"So maybe this isn't for you."

"No no, I'll give it a try."

I wonder if Charlie Parker ever went ice-skating.

She's looking at an article about some venerable building that's going to be torn down. A citizen's committee is protesting. Margot loves New York. She once told me she couldn't imagine living anywhere else. We approach the 42nd Street stop with plans to shuttle over to the east side but Margot says she knows of a great shoe store not too far up on Broadway.

"Let's go upstairs and get you some shoes."

"Let's not."

We go back and forth about it.

"I noticed your shoes last night. You'll get sick walking around in those shoes."

"I put in new cardboard. I'm cool."

"Surely you jest."

"Not really."

"This time of year everything is on sale. For a few bucks you can add a decade to your life."

"I won't let you buy me shoes."

"Why not?"

"It's going to mess up what's left of our sex life."

She chuckles but I'm serious.

"You can pay me back."

"I won't be able to."

"There's no hurry."

"They won't have my size."

"You never know."

"They just have those Italian dancing slippers with the pointy toe."

"Let's see."

"It's not a wise move."

"Why?"

"What's next? Me on the bottom? That kind of thing."

"What's wrong with being on the bottom?"

Margot is so naïve.

Richie will probably be happier if I moved out of 454. I wouldn't blame him. But I don't want to drag Margot down with any of that. She works all week and is trying to have some fun on the weekend. I will let her buy me a pair of shoes. It'll make her happy. Oooh Mel, so thoughtful.

We walk upstairs and up Broadway, passing the Strand where its blockbuster Christmas movie has just opened. The blurb speaks of this family's "wacky hijinks" and calls it "the zaniest hit of the season." Kate Cameron gives it four stars. Says it's "daffy." On the diagonal we cross Broadway mid-block, my arm around her shoulder, guiding her masculinely through the slow-moving traffic. We walk up to the window.

"Do you see anything you like?" she asks,

"Hmm. What about those black ones in the corner?"

"They're nice."

"They won't fit."

"Let's go in."

Back-to-back seats down the middle of the floor and a green wall-to-wall rug. A salesman approaches, feigning interest, civility, enthusiasm. You name it, he's feigning it.

"Afternoon, people."

Go-getter, his hair is thinning and he's overweight but powerful-looking. Wears a tie-clasp, shoe horn bending out of his breast pocket. Kind of guy who tells long jokes, swears by Buicks. Name's probably Angelo.

"I need shoes."

"Lucky for you, that's exactly what we sell here."

"Look, I'm not used to being the straight man. *I* get all the good lines."

Margot raises her hand like the Pope quieting the crowd.

"He needs shoes."

"Of course. Please have a seat. Dress shoe, work shoe?..."

"You got triple E?"

"Sure. Dress shoe. Work shoe?..."

"I was thinking of that black pair you have in the window. In the corner, toward the street."

"8505?"

"Well, maybe if you throw in a pair of socks."

"Ha ha that's the style number."

144

"Hm. Silly of me not to know the style number. Probably unforgivable."

"I'll check in back. Maybe we're in luck. Why don't you and your wife have a seat."

That has a nice ring to it.

"Yes, why don't you have a seat, Margot."

"Make yourselves at home. I'll be back in a flash."

Margot sits, zips open her jacket and crosses her black leotarded legs. He walks back and by us in the other direction.

"No can do but I think I've got something you'll like."

He's rustling around in the back room. A guy behind me trying on galoshes. Used to be my winter outfit was galoshes and my mackinaw. Good & Plenty in the balcony and the best speller around. He returns with a very corny number, white stitching around the sole and peanut brittle on top.

"I want a plain toe. I should've told you that. Just a plain Anglo-Saxon toe."

"I thought I'd show them to you. Wing-tips are always popular. We'll see what we shall see."

He's brisk and unflappable, in the back room again, whistling. I try to identify the tune but I can't. Maybe he's improvising. Margot lights up a Newport. The Danish-modern chair makes me feel fat. Back with another box, he draws up his little seat like a kid's portable shoeshine set-up and takes out a pair of canvas shoes which I kind of like even though he calls them desert casuals. When I take off my shoe, the cardboard, already kind of shredded, sticks to my socks and I brush it off on the rug.

"Natty I'm not."

"That's all right. At least it shows you're in the market for shoes…How do you like these?"

"They're cool, actually."

"How's the fit? It's 12 triple E."

"Let me get up and assume some natural every-day movements."

I walk over to the triptych mirror. I see I have a bit of a hooked nose. Not to mention an affinity for the cello. Dirty four-eyed Jew-bastard. On the anvil of western culture we forge an ethnocentric mercantilism and crowd the best beaches. At least we're not social problems like some other minorities I could mention. We're achievers. Most of us. Since I can't afford a nose-job I've cultivated all the gentile virtues. I'm obedient, modest, well-mannered, moderate, optimistic. I don't make waves. Mostly, though, I crave gentile women. That's how it goes when you're first-generation Jewish American. Not like our immigrant fathers who spent their lives lighting candles, eating in the kitchen, and sitting on the can with the Forward. From Sinai to the Bronx, the end of the millennium. I represent the Second (premature) Coming.

"What do you think, Margot?"

"I like them but it's up to you."

"Well, there's no doubt that they invest me with some measure of verve. At the same time, one man's verve is another man's frivolity."

"He'll probably go on like that for a while."

"Perfectly all right. Why should a man be in a hurry?"

He smiles, mediating very well, fooling around with his shoehorn and copping glances at Margot's leotarded legs. He's got a bit of gold in his teeth and very big hands, both of which suggest a penis larger than my own.

"How much *are* these desert casuals?"

"$14.75 plus tax."

I'm about to forget it but behind him Margot nods a yes.

"These aren't on sale?" I ask.

"No, not those. But it's an excellent shoe and very current."

"Current."

"Oh yes."

"Give me another minute to consider my role in society."

"Take your time....Can I show *you* something?"

"No, I'm just a spectator."

"I like your boots."

"Thank you."

"We have a number like it. Argonne?"

"I. Miller."

"Very nice."

He's actually got her foot in his big hairy hand. If we lived together I wouldn't have to pretend I didn't care who fucked her. We'd do the Sunday puzzle together, look for Nina in the Hirschfeld cartoon, leave funny little notes to each other.

"I've reached a decision."

They don't even hear me. She's got her fur-lined boot off and he's got his hand in it half way up his forearm. Why don't they just go into the back room and get it over with? It's an outrage.

"I'll take the shoes. If they're still for sale ha ha."

"Okie-dokie. You want to wear them out the door?"

"Yes."

He wants to lace them up for me and, god damn it, I let him. Now he walks behind the counter.

"No need wrapping the old shoes. You can throw them out if you wouldn't mind."

Margot zips up her jacket and takes a twenty out of her purse. She furtively gives me the bill and walks over to the mirror to check out her hair.

"With the tax it's $15.64."

He gives me the change and tells me to come back

again. He means with Margot, of course. Outside it's cold but the sun's blazing. I kiss her on the cheek and decide not to bring up her indiscretion with Angelo. As we stroll, we start talking about hot spots on the west side. I ask her if she's ever been to the Romanesque courtyard on 79th near the river. It's one of my favorite places. I'm a little surprised to find that she hasn't. All of a sudden she says, "I have an idea. Let's not go skating. We probably couldn't rent a set of parallel bars anyway. Let's go to the Romanesque courtyard instead."

"Serious?"

"Sounds like a great spot."

We walk back toward the subway station, Margot's arm in mine. Now she lets my arm go to blow her nose in the yellow Kleenex from her purse. I glance at her open purse and see her pack of Newports in its plastic case with a tiny compartment for the matches, her rain-hat folded into the size of a half-dollar, WQXR program guide, chapstick, paper-mate pen, calorie counter.

We pass a theater that's showing a musical, with a bunch of kids in a circle around two chaperones who are giving the kids instructions: stay in a group, no noise, etc. I remember a dramatic club junket from Milford High. We saw *Wish You Were Here* with this real swimming pool right in the stage and I was drunk in the balcony yelling for this girl I dug at the time, trying to find out where she was sitting. "Nancy, where are you?" The ushers started getting on me and finally tossed me out during the first act. I wandered around Times Square, hoping I'd live here some day.

While we're waiting for the red light at 44th Street, an elderly couple, out-of-towners, sidle up to us.

"Begging your pardon," she says to me, "could you please tell us the whereabouts of a restaurant called McGinnis'?"

"Drovya stash, mikyastopol grizhnev."

"I'm so sorry. We thought you were--"

Margot butts in. "It's around 48th and Broadway. Just three or four more blocks up Broadway."

"Oh, thank you so much."

"You're quite welcome."

"Are you two enjoying America?"

Boy, there's a loaded question.

"Uh, yes," Margot says. "Yes, we are."

"Byov, byev, byav."

"You say it's on 48th Street?"

"Maybe 49th. I can't remember. But you'll be close."

"I do appreciate your kindness. And allow me to say that you speak English beautifully."

"Thank you."

"Gorky, Gogol, Plisetskaya."

"Yes. Well goodbye and bless you both."

"Goodbye."

"Nyet."

They leave, the man touching the brim of his hat for Margot.

"How cruel and rude you can be. It amazes me."

"Oh, come on."

"She was such a sweet lady."

"She was a cop."

"There was no point to it. Just garden variety insensitivity." She shakes her head in frustration. "It's the shoes, isn't it? You're mad at me for buying you...my god."

Actually I was just trying to have some fun. We both retreat into silence. Hm, cruel and rude. Serious charges.

"I guess I should say I'm sorry."

"If you really thought that, you would just say it."

"I'm sorry."

She takes back my hand without saying anything and we head to the subway.

At 79th we walk down the path under the West Side Highway and then along the water's edge to the marina. The boats knock against each other and make little splashing sounds. There are a few others here, strolling around, but when we walk over to the courtyard it's empty and the fountain is turned off.

The sun is still bright but lower now and the high round walls of the courtyard keep it out. Margot stretches out on the concrete bench and lays her head on my lap. She smiles at me. Living together would be the best way to be unhappy. Anyway, I'm tired of trying to figure everything out, especially since I'm so ill-equipped for the task.

"It's nice here," she says.

"Not many people know about this place."

"Are your hands cold?"

"A little."

"You need gloves."

"Oh it'll be spring in three months."

"Put your hands under my collar."

"All right."

We're in love with each other and don't even know it.

Out of the blue Margot starts chatting me up about my abortive novel.

She says, "Have you ever thought of writing a different kind of novel, one that you can feel happy about, instead of, you know, miserable?"

"You've just defined hack literature."

"Come on, Mel. There are two or three things in life that you want and they're the same two or three things that everyone wants...You'll just have to face it.

You're like everyone else."

She's right. We really could make it work.

"I'm thinking we should live together."

That seemed to have stopped the flow.

"You mean at *my* place?"

"Yeah."

Forehead maneuvers. Eyebrows rising. Now she's getting up and walking over to the fountain. High drama all of a sudden. After a minute I walk over to her and sit on the fountain wall, looking up at her. She's profoundly depressed.

She looks down at me and says, "Why?"

"Because I love you."

She greets these words, the first time I've uttered them to her, with silence, then:

"Mel, I have to maintain my independence. It's all I have."

"Hm."

"I need emotional security. You can't give me that."

"Okay."

"What I want is legitimate. I love you too but I've got to take better care of myself."

"Okay."

"Also, I'd be supporting you and liking it because I'd think I'd have some power over you and I'd grow to hate myself for that and probably you too."

"Okay."

"Let's face it, you don't want to go on living at 454 and you've run out of ideas...We'd be miserable living together."

"Sorry I brought it up."

"Oh Mel," she says.

Boy, that truly was a terrible idea. And what kind of weakness made me utter those words? But now I know that she dug me the way I was. Namely, not around much. I, stupidly, wanted more. This on again-off again stuff is sometimes the only way that some relationships can exist. She doesn't want a cleaned-up me, and I don't want a new improved her. She's perfect. And so am I. I just got greedy.

Now she walks to the other side of the fountain. She's crying and doesn't want me to notice. She turns and looks at me. All of a sudden it's cold and getting dark, the darkness smudging her into the gray rock wall, her eyes and hands mica crystals. Desculpted, back where she came from.

Margot thinks she ought to leave. Sure, anything else would be anti-climactic. Walking across West End Avenue she waves at a cab and he squeals over to us. I expect her to smile bravely but she doesn't. She stares at me, just like Marie Gagliardi on the subway platform. We're both getting more inaccessible each second. She disappears in the cab and takes off as the sound-track rises. The whole world is a cinder in my eye.

Chapter Eight

I walk the 37 streets back to 454, thinking about my book and that, no matter what, I have to finish it. Probable title: The Lance Blatt Story. The movie will star John Cassavetes and Tuesday Weld. Sidney Lumet will direct. Kate Cameron will give it one star, call it arty and sordid.

The super is buffing the lobby. Saturday night and he's buffing the lobby. What's *his* life like? The long rubber carpet is all rolled up, holding the door open.

"Hi, Mr. Schein."

"Don't track in."

"I just got new shoes. Nothing sticks to them yet."

"I waxed. Don't rub in the heels."

Not even a hello. Only my legendary good manners prevent me from telling him to go fuck himself.

G. Gormley should be here again in January, testing the cables and the pulleys. The elevator slows down at the 11th floor, as is its wont, and takes its good time getting to the 12th floor. G. Gormley may be here in January, but I won't.

At the door I take out the wrong key. Margot's. In the same pocket, change from the twenty for the shoes. Four singles, two quarters, a dime, four pennies. That'll cover laundry, cigarettes, subway fare, wint-o-mint life savers, Times, coffee, two knishes from Merit Farms, a ham salad sandwich at the Senator cafeteria and a matinee at the Nemo. I walk in and it's dark like no one's home, except there's a light from the kitchen and when I walk in Richie is in his overcoat, kneeling down to the open stove. Did I catch him in the nick of time? No, he's basting a chicken. He looks up at me, then back again, getting under the wings with the back of the wooden spoon. He pushes in the rack, closes the oven door and stands up. I'm girding my loins.

"Smells funny," I say.

"It's the sage."

"Where is everybody?"

"Out. Who knows."

"I want to apologize for last night."

"You're forgiven."

"I had a speech."

"Save it."

"For the movie version?"

"Of course."

"Thanks for not rubbing my nose in it."

"You're welcome."

"Have you seen Getz?"

"I called him about an hour ago."

"How'd it go?"

"He was very civil and extremely understanding, and you know what that means."

"It could mean you're--"

"It means I'm *out,* as in out of his *life*...I said maybe early next week we could meet and talk things over. Early, middle, late, he's *booked*. And the following week he'll be in New Haven trying to save what's-his-face's play and then blah blah fucking blah."

"I couldn't feel worse."

"Yeah," Richie says meditatively. Then: "What you did killed me but on the other hand I might've done the same thing. I trust you got in some zingers."

"I was pretty smashed but yeah, a couple."

"He probably deserved every word...There was a can of creamed corn."

"Second shelf. By the graham crackers."

"You hungry?"

"Nah."

"I thought you were with Margot today."

"Who's Margot?"

He gives me a sympathetic look. Damn, he really has forgiven me. *He* actually feels bad for *me*.

"Eat some chicken," he says.

"Maybe later. Save me some."

"I'm gonna eat the whole chicken?"

"I'm thinking of leaving."

"Where you going?"

"Hmm. San Francisco?"

"Why?"

"I'm going crazy here"

"Is that all?"

"I'm not doing anything. I just hang around..."

"Where's the can opener?"

"...In the sink. Norman depresses me, Marty hates me, Alex reminds me of Milford."

"And me?"

"You feed me and pay my rent which makes me feel like a bum. I'm a bum."

"We're all bums."

"Okay then, I'm a bigger bum. I'm the biggest bum in New York."

"You're the only bum I can talk to."

"I can't support myself. I can't write my book. I can't get out of the *rain*. I'm pathetic."

"I'll make my movie and we'll be rich."

"I don't want to be your Tonto."

"What Tonto? I mean we'll have money. I'll hire you as a screenwriter hyphen casting director. But first things first. Throw me over those pot-holders....Hey, is that a bird or what?"

"What do you want, a review?"

"And these larger-than-life spuds."

He lugs out the big casserole dish and puts it on the table on two trivets. You'd think he'd get a spot on his overcoat. You'd think he'd take the damn thing off. It's two hundred degrees in here. He sets down two plates, then folds two napkins on the diagonal, lays forks and knives on them. Richie's already back on the horse.

"Eat."

"I'll have a leg. But no creamed corn."

"How many potatoes?"

"No potatoes."

"Have a small one."

"All right, a small one."

We eat quietly for a while.

"Margot and I are phffft."

"That's too bad. I really like Margot."

"Yeah. I'm already thinking of using some of the gory details in my novel. Lance Blatt started out having a nice thing with his girlfriend Gretchen. Out of the goodness of my heart I gave him a nice thing, and then he blows it by starting a fight with her over nothing. By chapter three they're splitsville. But what can you say about a guy who's writing a novel about a guy who's writing a novel about a guy who's writing a novel?"

"I never mentioned it before but I never liked the name Gretchen for his girlfriend. I picture a big blond

Nordic chick with pigtails. What about Elaine or something?"

"You're probably right. Maybe Lance could relate better to a chick named Elaine."

"No question about it."

"I'm sick of dealing with the ridiculous Lance Blatt. I'm close to just giving up the whole project. He's so fucked up and cynical it's almost funny. And if the book ever did get published the critics'll hate it. First novels are the most patronized works of art. I could write the review: The Lance Blatt Story is a self-pitying, coming-of-age yawner, predictably immature and self-absorbed, replete with interior monologues that substitute for plot, obscure literary references (the last refuge of a minor talent) and look-ma-no-hands sentence construction. So there you are. The critics also told Keats he should've stayed in med school. And they were right. The world doesn't deserve *Ode on a Grecian Urn*. Or Grecian Oin, as Norman would say. "

"Man, you are so hung up...all your bitches are with life and the past and all that shit. You know there's no such thing as life or the past. Or art or mankind or God."

"So what is there?"

"You really don't know, do you?"

"No. I don't."

I really don't.

"There's this chicken, for starters...deep, right?" and he starts wailing on one of the legs.

160

I created all this. Richie, Margot, even the creamed corn. And now I don't want it.

Richie rises and rinses his hands at the sink. "I gotta run. I have a date with Rothman's secretary. She knows Saul Wittstein's daughter, so between the two of them I hope to get a meet with Wittstein's partner, Luckman, who I might have mentioned is a big investor. He's more into plays than movies but I'll love him and he'll love me."

Damn, this is where I came in.

"And I love his name. Hold on. Maybe it *is* Sid Luckman."

I was wrong about Richie. I was wrong about everything. I wish he would've been mad at me. That would have been easier. That would've forced the action. Now *I've* got to force the action.

He walks out of the kitchen and I follow him. At the door he says, "You won't leave, will you?"

"Good luck with Rottstein or whatever the fuck his name is."

He slaps his wallet pocket, slaps his breast pocket, smoothes his hair back, checks his gloves, throws his arms out and asks me how he looks. I tell him he looks good because I have uttered my last joke, the last witty hyphen pithy remark of my life.

As soon as the door closes my heart starts pounding. I turn the darkroom lights on. The heart. I turn the hall light on. No one in Richie's room, in

Marty's room, in Alex's room. I turn all the lights on. In the living room I see the Riverside lights, the Jersey lights, the lit-up ALCOA sign. Looking for the right record. Beethoven too emotional, Stravinsky too intellectual, Charlie Parker too stark, Bach too deep. The radio. Vic Damone. Perfect. A vein jerks my top lip. Another vein starts ticking on the back of my right wrist. Another vein out from under the middle fingernail of my left hand. I try to knead it away but I can't. I rub it along my leg but it keeps pulsating. I used to take my father's carpenter's level and check everything in the house to see if it was level. When I stand still my body hums and bumps, my heart pumping. I remember she said everyone's bad the first time. How are you the *second* time? My heart is trying to break out of the jail of my ribs. Afraid of dying, of being dead like everything else. Like the coffee table from dead trees. Books by dead men. Can't stay still. I roll on the floor to shake it off. On the straw mat I rip a straw tube from the mat. Keep my fingers busy. Cracking the yellow straw, work it between my thumb and index finger, rubbing it down to the gray nap, crushing it into powder, grinding the powder in my fingers and into my skin. Straw, white Moby Dick walls, dead table, carcass, carrion, corpse. Couldn't recognize you now if I dug up the ground and broke into where you are. Just an open wound with a million creeping things sucking your insides. You're just a pulp. Nothing left of you but yellowing photographs and my book that I can't write. Your father has expired. You must've been lonely after mama died. Why didn't you tell me?

162

You knew you would die before me. Why didn't you tell me what to do? That's all right. I'm not angry, We fought so much. Let's not fight now. Sometimes you slapped me in the face, huh? That's okay, I cried for a while but you were just being my father, trying your best. Remember that time when I got big and you tried to slap me but I grabbed you by both wrists and pinned your arms back. I was bigger and stronger than you. You didn't mind. You were my father and I was your son and that's all that mattered. What was the last second like? Did you think of me? Did you think of mama? Did you think of Poland? Did you think of someone I never heard of from long ago, someone you always remembered and never told anyone about? Were you afraid? I know you were alone even though I was there. Just like I'm alone now with nothing left to say, no one to say goodbye to, no one to say I'm sorry to, no one to say I love you to. Nothing to do but die.

A vein on my kneecap. A vein in my throat, behind my eyes. My glasses fall off my face but the blur is good. The blur keeps the heart back. I put the glasses back on and the throbbing starts again. I take them off and it calms down. It's the glasses. It's always been the glasses. Everything too sharp. Too literal. The outline of things cuts the world to ribbons. Keep the glasses off. It's okay.

I want to throw the glasses out the window but I chicken out. Lance Blatt would throw them out the window but they're the only ones I have and I might need them. I'll just put them on the coffee table. The room relaxes. No sharp borders, nothing defined.

163

Could I start again right here? Oh if I could just be a poor monk in India who's not afraid of dying. No such thing as the past, no such thing as art. I should go out and look around. Saturday night in the city.

The coat's in the kitchen. I take the dishes off the table and put them in the sink. I hit a glass on the faucet and it breaks, and when I finger around for the pieces I cut my thumb. I rinse my thumb with warm water and suck the blood. A minor and insignificant mishap. I wrap my cum-stained handkerchief around my thumb and the bleeding stops after a minute. Okay, let's go.

Down the elevator and when the door opens I find that the buffing machine is still in the lobby. I know this because I bump into it. I look in the direction of Mr. Schein who's either smiling or frowning. For the same price, as my father used to say, I choose to believe he's smiling.

"Hello, Mr. Schein."

"Watch the cord."

I feel it ride over my shoe and tighten against my ankle, then loosen. I've pulled out the plug. I make a gesture to grab the cord but he yanks it in his hand and plugs it in again which is best because I would have trouble finding the socket. I walk out in the middle of his mumble, and I'm careful on the slippery steps. On Riverside Drive headlights run along a shooting-gallery in both directions like on the Nemo movie marquee. There's very little wind at The Corner which surprises me. I was ready for it, too. Up on Broadway I need to cross the street. Safer at night. You can see headlights. But in the curb is a deep puddle and my right foot steps in it over my brand new desert casual, freezing my foot. I get back on the sidewalk, lean against a parked car and take off my shoe so I can squeeze out my sock. I squeeze and squeeze and the sock, once soaken wet, is now just damp. I put on my sock and shoe and dry my hands with my cummy, bloody handkerchief. This time I jump over the puddle but I wasn't watching for cars that zip down Broadway. The brakes squeal and the car misses me but I have to jump away and I fall down on my elbow. Guy gets out of his car and yells to the guy bent over me, "I didn't hit him. There was no contact. You saw that. You're a witness."

The guys says, "Honestly I couldn't say either way."

My elbow really hurts and I don't care that I'm stretched out in the middle of the wet street.

"You ran right in front of me…What's the matter?"

"My elbow."

"You ran right in front of me."

"I know. It wasn't your fault."

To the other guy he says, "You heard that. You heard him say it wasn't my fault."

"I told you, I couldn't say either way."

"But you heard him *say* it wasn't his fault. You're a witness to *that,* right?"

"I ain't saying anything. This man is hurt."

"You got ears, don't you?"

"Why do you need a witness? I admitted it was my fault."

"You may change your mind when you see your lawyer."

My lawyer? Now he's running around asking everyone to be a witness. I better get out of here.

The other guy asks me how my elbow is. Then he says, "Try to stand. You'll catch pneumonia on the sidewalk."

This cat is a fucking saint. I hear someone say a cop is coming over. I sit up. The cop stands over me, an archipelago of buttons and badges that glint.

"You okay?"

"I hurt my elbow but I'm okay."

"You gonna need an ambulance?"

"No no."

The driver says there was no contact. Is that true?"

"Yes it is. I fell getting out of the way but it was my fault, not his. I wasn't looking."

I push myself up, the good guy helping me. The cop tells everyone to "disperse." The good guy is going to cross the street too so we walk across together. A very safe feeling, walking across the street together.

"Keep bending the elbow so it doesn't stiffen up on you," he tells me.

"Thanks. You're the only one who gave a shit."

"People are afraid."

That's very true. I know *I'm* afraid.

"What's your name?"

"Wyatt."

"I'm Mel. Thanks for helping."

I want to keep walking with this guy but he stops in front of Riker's. He's going in for coffee and asks me to join him. I decide not to. Great guy but I'd have to tell him the story of my life and I don't think he'd understand. People that don't know me wouldn't understand. People that *do* know me wouldn't understand, either. Ophelia didn't understand. Even Horatio didn't really understand.

Crossing 114th, looking both ways and checking the curb. Yesterday I walked down this same street, past Salter's, past Gristedes, past Riker's, past the Take-Home Market, past Prexy's, past the West End, and in twenty-four hours I've ripped the skin off the world, and now everything is a running sore. At 113th three or four others start crossing. I sidle up to them and cross with them. Now I walk close to the storefronts to keep my bearing and avoid the confusion that reigns in the middle of the wide sidewalk. Sigmund Freud had agoraphobia. When I approach Gristedes I hit my head on the metal crossbar of the awning and my brain bangs against the padded walls of my head, shaking like maracas. This hurts worse than my elbow. I fall to one knee, then to both knees, holding my head, thumbs across my ears. This might make me insane. I remember that guy from Milford, Sid Danzig, the director of the park & rec department. He fell down the steps of the Milford Town Hall and six months later split his wife's head open with an axe.

It must look like I'm praying here, kneeling in the snow. I should be praying. That would make everything a lot easier. Easier but weirder. Someone's tapping my shoulder, now rubbing it, but my mouth won't open.

"You all right?"

I'm hurt and depressed and I could go on but I guess you could say I'm all right. You'd really have to define all right. I need to talk to every person I've ever known and explain everything to them, tell them that they were very important to me, that I loved them and I wanted them to love me but I was too afraid to show it. Afraid of the dismantling of Lemuel Pitkin because I knew it was about me or would be some day if I stayed in this city and now that day is here.

"I'm fine, thanks," I say. Sure. Fine.

"Why don't you try standing up.."

"Hey, isn't that the same guy who was hit by that car?"

"The car didn't hit him. He fell getting out of the way."

"Oh. He's holding his head. He must've hurt his head."

"How could he hurt his head. I think he's just depressed or something."

"Maybe getting hit by the car had a delayed reaction."

168

"I told you, the car didn't hit him."

"It must've hit him. Let's call a cop."

I grab his hand and make the long climb up his arm until I'm standing. Both of them are short. How could they imagine anyone banging his head on Gristedes' awning?

"No cop," I say. "See, I'm just depressed. My girlfriend left me and I can't get her back because I realize I'm not worthy of her and I'd only make her unhappy."

"Maybe if you talked to her one more time and told her how you felt..."

"I'd have to invent a whole new person. *Two* persons."

"You going to be okay?"

I'm not sure but I'll assume an antic disposition. No one will notice if I'm "okay" or not.

A few others have gathered, keeping their distance but checking out the scene. They also wonder if I'm "okay" and they all finally agree that I am. We all "disperse" again.

Lots of cars passing in both lanes with an occasional pididdle. In Milford, when you saw a pididdle you were supposed to kiss the girl next to you, if there was a girl next to you, which was usually not the case. At 112th I wait for the cars. When they all go by, the others cross but I stand there for three or four more batches of cars. Where am I going that I'm in such a hurry to get run over at every corner. I'm soaking wet, walking around with a cracked head and a maybe a broken elbow. The thousand natural shocks.

I decide to walk back toward Riker's. I want to find that guy Wyatt and properly thank him. And now the ghost of my father walks up to me and looks at me with a troubled forehead and asks me, What do you want? My father, back from the dead, bicycle clip pincushion on his wrist, his collar tips rolled up because he always forgot the stays, this same person and no doubt about it, my father, cap a pie, come back to tell me that it only hurts when you laugh and keep your eye on that nurse with the morphine. She'll tell you how well you're looking but don't believe her, you look lousy and before she hangs up that dextrose bottle and puts the oxygen mask over your face, better touch her, do something, because it's all over. You don't know it but it is.

I can't just scan the counter so I bend over each shoulder to get a good look. They look back at me but I can't read their thoughts. Not that I could when I wore glasses, when I thought I knew everything. I come to the end of the U-shaped counter. He's not there. I don't think I missed him but it's hard to tell. There are lots of booths but he'd probably be at the counter.

I yell "Wyatt" pretty loud. Heads swivel toward me and the fry cook asks me what I want. I yell "Wyatt" again. Loud enough for him to hear if he was still there. This time no heads turn. But now the fry cook asks me again what is going on and he sounds miffed.

"I'm looking for a guy named Wyatt."

"What's he look like?"

"I don't really know."

"C'mon, man, don't cause a disturbance."

"I won't. Don't call a cop."

"Don't worry. Just stop yelling."

"Okay. I'm a little fucked up right now."

"Your head's got blood on it."

"No, I mean inside."

"Go over to St. Luke's. They'll fix you up."

"No, man. Inside, inside."

"What do you need?"

"Nothing. Everything. But mostly nothing."

"Sit down and have some coffee."

The waitress yells in burger orders.

The fry cook walks away to push down the toaster and throw stuff on the grill. He's another good guy, but he's there and I'm here. My sleeve catches on a lever of the cigarette machine. I walk past all the backs, some of them turning to me but no one says anything or touches me. He wasn't there. Outside on the sidewalk with nowhere to go.

Near 116th I can see three guys ready to cross Broadway. I get there just in time and make it to the esplanade with them but then they start running to beat the light and I lose them. On the esplanade now, in the middle of Broadway. The cars shoot by like torpedoes. I hear the downtown train underneath me through the grating as it heads out of the 116th Street station. I'm waiting for the green light but why I don't know. When I get across, then what?

The grating has no snow on it, melted by the steam from the train, so I lie down on it and find it's not uncomfortable. The clouds are gone and there are a million stars. So beautiful. I guess this is what Alex calls The Macrocosm. I don't see the sky that often, especially at night. It's not that kind of town. Suddenly I'm very tired. It's peaceful at the end, when there isn't anything to go back to. I might as well relax and let the universe have its way with me. I never trusted the universe before, which is funny. C'mon, the universe *knows* stuff...The stars don't have that sharp outline they usually have. Without my glasses the stars look like when dandelions go to seed and turn into those white fluffy things that you blow off and watch them float around. Did it all start in the second grade when we lined up along the wall for recess and I heard Reggie Van Etten say to the kid in front of him, "I hope Hitler kills *all* the Jews"? Or did it all end there? But that wasn't the first time I was really scared. I was scared when we were still living in the Bronx, when mom and dad dropped me off at camp north of the city for a whole week, where I didn't know anyone or get to know anyone and I was too afraid to take a shower with the other kids. That's where I learned to tie my shoelaces and they gave me a star, actually a sticker in the shape of a star, on an official-looking piece of paper, which meant a lot to me. Was it that week that I got all fucked up? When I discovered loneliness? When I became *me*? Every little thing, every step along the way turned out to be crucial. No one warned me about that. Like on New Year's Eve in my freshman year in high school, this good looking girl, Judy Pawlecki, a *sophomore*, didn't have a date and was baby-sitting not far from where I lived on Seaside Avenue. I didn't know her that well so I surprised myself as well as her when I walked over there and knocked on the door. We sat on the couch and listened to some records. I got up enough nerve to kiss her. She was okay with that but I wasn't sure about the next step so I left it alone. That next step has always been a problem. I sang her a song—*Dream a Little Dream of Me*. She dug that. Singing a song has always seemed the right thing to do. I used to love singing with Stewie, Tony, Danny and a few other guys on Bayview beach and on the street in downtown Milford—rock & roll and folk and pop and doo-wop. It's when I'm not singing that everything seems a bit off, like that blond whore who wouldn't take off her bustier. Or Cindy Golden when we were playing spin the bottle and I spun the bottle and it pointed to her, who only dated high school guys when she was in the eighth grade, and college guys when she was in high school, who I fantasized about in class, and who was wearing a white clingy dress, and when we went into the next room to be alone and have our kiss and I put my arms around her waist, she laughed. Oh, I know, everybody's fucked up. I'm not the only one. I'm just the only one who is *me*. I can't say I did my best because I've never done my best. And I got what I deserved, which is nothing. My final regret is that I didn't tell my story, because that's important. And there are only a few things that are really important. I sorta tried with Lance Blatt except that I'm not Lance Blatt. I'm Mel Montrose and I can only tell The Mel Montrose Story. Such as it is. I think our revels really *are* now ended. The actors, myself included, are melted into thin air, and so is the action, the ideas, the emotions, all dissolved, leaving nothing behind because we really *are* such stuff as dreams are made of. Right now I just want to be left alone so that I can think the purest thoughts I've ever thought. Did I mention I'm very tired, tired of myself mostly, and I need to rest and stay right here on this surprisingly comfortable grating...and our little life is rounded with a sleep...

Coda

The pilot just announced that our altitude is 32,000 feet. Shit, man, that's about six *miles*. I feel like Buck Rogers. This is my first time in a plane. Where have *I* been? When I look at the stewardesses I wonder if Marty's ever dated any of them. Hard to believe I almost died on Saturday night and here it is Wednesday afternoon, four days later, and I'm not only alive but finally making the break.

When I woke up early Sunday afternoon I noticed a lot of blood on my pillow case. My head was still sore, and my elbow too. This cop woke me up and told me I had to get off the grating. I was sleeping like a baby but I was real cold. The cop said I probably would've frozen to death if he hadn't woken me up, that it was almost 4:00 in the morning, and that people freeze to death on the streets every night during the winter. He said, you gotta keep moving. Not bad advice, I thought. I took it to heart.

First thing I did when I got out of bed was to find my glasses, which were right where I left them the night before—on the coffee table in the living room—so I could read my address book, and *find* my address book. As it happened only Norman spent the night at the flat and was still asleep. Alex must've spent the night at Jane's. Marty was with a stewardess or a nurse. Richie probably got lucky and spent the night at what's-his-name's secretary's place.

I finally got the number I needed and called this cat Don in San Fran. He came through like a champ, said he had an extra room and to stay as long as I wanted. The next day I sold my father's moonstone ring for a hundred and fifty dollars at a pawn shop on Amsterdam Avenue. The "midnight special" plane ticket was ninety-nine so I even have a few bucks to buy Don a beer. I think I'm happy.

San Francisco is a tabula rasa. I can re-write my life, edit out all the bad shit. I used to think a lot about my father leaving Poland and traveling all the way to New York to make a life for himself. That must've been hard. But he stayed right there on the east coast. He

175

never traveled west of the Hudson River. And then he had a son, me, who's finally going west of the Hudson River, way west, as far west as you can go in this country, and someday I'll have a son and he'll probably go on to China or some shit. The species evolves, man. It really does.

I said my goodbyes to Richie, Alex, Norman, Marty, and I called Margot and said goodbye to her. They were all shocked that I was actually making the move but wished me well. I wonder when or even *if* I'll ever see them on the west coast. Yeah, you never know, but they're all such hardcore New Yorkers. Meaning they've gotten used to the harsh winters and the nuttiness.

I look down out my window and see clouds—the *tops* of clouds. I'm somewhere over the rainbow.

Mel Montrose: Live at the Carleton!

A couple of months after I arrived in San Francisco I had a place on the west slope of Russian Hill, right on the Hyde Street cable-car line. The ad called it "cozy," one room with a Murphy bed, kitchenette, tiny bathroom. The building was called The Carleton. It had five floors and an elevator. I lived on the fourth floor.

New York had worn me out. I was a wreck after my parents died, and those winters were severe. Instead of playing the cards I had been dealt, I decided to throw them in and get a whole new hand. The night before I left, Margot said, "You really think you can just walk away from it all?"

Frisco was rough at first. I stayed with my buddy Don for two weeks but I felt I was crowding him a bit so for the next month or so I lived downtown in buck-a-night pensioner hotels like the St. Regis at Fourth and Market, where the Marriott is now. I ate at missions south of Market where they make you listen to the sermon before you get the food. I scanned the curbs of Market Street for long-ish cigarette butts. I left that style behind after I got my first job--bussing tables at Foster's Cafeteria on Polk and Sutter.

I used to haunt the clubs in North Beach. For a while I was singing Friday and Saturday nights with the house band, usually a quintet, at a place then called The Boheem. Those guys could play. They didn't know what to make of me at first. Between sets one night I walked into a room behind the bar where they hung out, and before they had a chance to ask me what the hell I needed, I asked them if I could sit in, one tune. I threw a chart on the table they were sitting at—*Tadd's Delight*, a Tadd Dameron tune I had written words to. Without saying much else, we just went back out there and did it. I thanked them and was ready to jump off the set when the tenor player asked me to call out another tune. Well, okay. We wound up doing a few more and that's how I got to sing with the band.

We began by rehearsing once or twice a week but soon we stopped and just showed up for the gig. The problem was that singing on Fridays and Saturdays wasn't enough. In the few months I'd been in town I hadn't met many musicians, or anybody else, for that matter. What I started doing was singing with a metronome, an old electric one that just did fit into the suitcase that I brought with me. Maybe I was lonely, but the metronome became like a friend. That pulse propelled a rhythm section, a big band, a string ensemble, whatever I needed. Just a boy and his metronome. I had always sung by myself for fun. Now I was singing by myself with a purpose, experimenting with my voice, learning new tunes, listening more to my phrasing.

I worked at Foster's from 11:00 in the morning to 7:00. One night I came home after my shift and whipped out my metronome, set it on a real slow tempo, and started to sing *You Don't Know What Love Is*, a tune running through my head all day. On the third word--"know"--I was aware of footsteps from the apartment above *stopping*. That is, I wasn't aware of the footsteps until they stopped. Since I moved in I had occasionally heard footsteps from above, but they never stopped like that just as I began to sing. Until that moment I had never even thought about who lived there. It was probably a single person and someone who wasn't home often. Suddenly, I was curious: male or female? It wasn't a heavy enough step to indicate male. Probably a female or a diminutive male.

Sensing that I had an audience made me give more of myself. That one person upstairs, like that solitary pulse, was all I needed. It was only after I turned *You Don't Know What Love Is* inside out, sustaining the last note until my breath was spent, that I allowed myself to think that maybe, probably, no one was listening. The footsteps just happened to stop when I started singing. Or maybe the person heard but doesn't dig music, or digs music but just doesn't care.

Before I figured out what I wanted to do about it, I first had to prove that someone upstairs really was listening. For the next three nights I came straight home instead of stopping for a beer at the Tiki Room on Sutter as I usually did. I stood by my table and listened. Zip. Nobody home. She could be asleep. See, it was a she already. On the fourth day I returned home at the same time, around 7:30, and there they were--footsteps, light as usual. I got right to work. I set the metronome on a ballad tempo. I was aware of my heartbeat, about three beats for each pock. Meanwhile the footsteps had stopped. Now I had to wait until they started again. I turned off the metronome so I could hear better. I stood there wondering how many minutes or hours I would wait before giving up. Then I heard the footsteps. I turned the metronome back on and pushed the on-button.

Young and Foolish, why was it wrong to be...

The footsteps stopped right after "foolish."

Young and Foolish, we haven't long to be.
Soon enough the carefree days, the sunlit days go by.
Soon enough a bluebird wants to fly.

On "fly" I pressed my finger on the metronome's stop button and let loose an extended bit of melisma that I didn't know I had in me. I released the button. Pock pock pock...

We were foolish. One day we fell in love.
Now I wonder what we were dreaming of.
Smiling in the sunlight, laughing in the rain,
I wish that we were Young and Foolish again.

I stopped the metronome and stood there listening. No sound above me. Nothing. I waited about ten seconds more before the footsteps started again. Whoever it was had stopped and listened to the whole thing, then probably just stood there waiting like I did. She probably got tired of doing that and walked away. Maybe she got thirsty or had to go to the bathroom.

Okay, someone was listening. Now I should want to know who, but I already began to think of the person upstairs as my muse. Yes, a beautiful woman, musically gifted, soulful, the whole bit. No reality could match that. I became obsessed with *not* wanting to know.

I stood to lose my muse just for the outside shot at Boom City.

For the next few nights I went through the usual ritual. I got all ready, waited for the footsteps, and pushed the metronome's on-button. Then I launched into my A set, my B set, my ballad set, my bebop set, my Matt Dennis set, like that. "Mel Montrose—Live at the Carleton!" It gave me new strength, too. I would scat fifty choruses of the blues and double-time all the ballads. Once I knew that one person--male or female-- was there, *listening*, I could open up.

Funny, though, how a puny thing like curiosity can overwhelm all other considerations. One Monday night I was walking back from work and I noticed a stunning, well-dressed woman ahead of me walk up the steps of my building and open her mailbox. It appeared to be the second, third, or fourth mailbox from the left on the top row. I picked up my pace, wanting to ride up in the elevator with her to find out where she got off, but I wasn't quick enough. I charged up the steps, three at a time, and heard the elevator stop at the second floor. That gave me enough time to beat the elevator up to the fifth floor, but it never arrived. I was breathing hard and I knew I was hooked.

I wasn't comfortable anymore singing to my audience of one. That person did inspire me but I needed more now, or would even settle for less. I took to waiting on a stoop across the street for long stretches. I even called in sick once to keep my vigil during the hours I normally worked. I stayed in great shape by running up the five flights fairly often. Occasionally a tenant would get off on the fifth floor but no one went to the apartment—5A--just above me.

One night I came home, got right into the routine I had perfected for a couple of weeks, and sat there in silence until I finally heard the footsteps. This time I walked quickly out of the apartment and ran up the stairs to the fifth floor. I walked right up to 5A and knocked three times.

After a bit I was about to turn away, thinking that he, she or it wasn't going to answer--maybe the three loud knocks were a bit much--when the doorknob turned and the door opened slowly. Through the four-inch opening of the door that was still chained I beheld a shriveled old woman looking up at me. Her eyes sparkled.

"Hi, I live in the room below you."

She stared at me. So this was my muse?

"I was wondering if my hi-fi was too loud for you."

She kept staring at me, then slowly shook her head sideways and smiled a tiny bit.

"Oh, that's good. I was worried about that."

My voice was too loud. I had seen enough and had backed up a couple of steps preparing to leave when she said, *whispered*, "My name is Greta Lasker. And yours?"

"Mel Montrose. Nice to meet you."

I thought she was closing the door on me and I felt relieved but it was only to release the chain. The door opened wide and she offered her small hand. I stepped forward and squeezed it much too hard.

"Please come in."

There was that whisper again, with a strong European accent. I wanted to make a getaway but the thought of being in her apartment, right over mine, intrigued me. She offered me some tea but I told her no thanks, I'd just be staying a minute. She gestured for me to sit on the couch as she sat down in a rocking chair. Her place had the exact same layout as mine. It was furnished about the same, too--minimally. I have a photo of my parents. She had no photos.

"No, your hi-fi doesn't disturb me," she said, still whispering. "I'm often playing my own records, so it's hard to hear anything else."

She pointed to her record player right by her on the end table. It was one of those old beat-up suitcase-looking things. There were a few records that were also within arm's reach. The record facing out was *Madame Butterfly*.

Just to make conversation: "I see you like opera."

"Yes, I used to sing."

"Really?"

She must've overdone it. Her pipes were shot.

"Did you sing in operas?"

"Oh yes." And then, smiling, "Many of them."

"Do you have laryngitis?"

"No. My vocal cords are damaged. Are you sure I can't get you something to drink?"

That touched a nerve. Chloe once told me that I sang all wrong. I didn't breathe right. I sang from my chest and constricted my throat. I was ruining my vocal cords.

"How did you hurt your vocal cords? Was it from singing?"

"No."

I was relieved.

"The Nazis experimented on me," she said, flashing her tiny smile again.

"You mean in a concentration camp?"

"Yes."

"Gee, that's horrible...how long were you there?"

"Two years."

"That's terrible. I'm so sorry."

"They killed my father, my husband and our son...many others, too, of course."

We both just sat there.

"I'm Polish. I sang at opera houses in Paris, Berlin, Vienna, Rome. The doctors at the camp all knew who I was. In fact, most of them were amateur musicians. They performed a series of experiments on my vocal cords...They were family men who thought they were doing great things for science."

"It must be hard to talk about."

"Not talking about it is harder."

"Sorry if I ever disturbed you from downstairs."

"Actually, I've never heard you."

"Good...You've never heard me?"

"No."

"You never heard me singing?"

"No. Do you sing? How nice."

Could this be my mother, in a rare instance of returning from the dead? It struck me that I, who thought I knew a thing or two, knew nothing. I was relieved to be unburdened of all the bogus knowledge I had accumulated. Mama, is that you? I thought of asking her where in Poland she was from but was afraid that she would say Lodz.

"You remind me of my mother."

She smiled.

"She's dead."

She kept the same smile through the silence until she said, "I'll be your mother if you want me to."

"You'll be my mother?"

"Yes. A mother is an older woman who cares about you."

I got up and walked over to her, thinking that I had better leave. She raised her two hands to take mine in what I thought was a parting gesture but as soon as I held her hands and felt a slight tug, I fell to my knees and buried my head in her lap. I cried for a long time. Longer than when I was a kid and got slapped by my father and sent to my room. I fell asleep. When I woke up I was in 4A, not 5A, on my couch. It was 11:15 and I was late for work.

On Friday nights at The Boheem, the first set usually has a smallish house. After three instrumentals I went up to do my first tune and noticed a couple of regulars who said hello. I tried to look at every person sitting there and at the bar, too. It was too dark to see most of them.

"I'd like to dedicate this set--and my life, too, while I'm at it--to a beautiful woman named Greta."

Behind me I heard the tenor player say to the trumpet player, "Looks like Mel's finally gettin' some."

All business, I turned and counted out a medium tempo.

> Without a song, the day would never end.
> Without a song, the road would never bend.
> When things go wrong a man ain't got a friend
> Without a song...

Nicole

My first jobs in San Francisco were a day here and a day there at various Foster's Cafeterias around the city. I worked at the ones on 7th and Market, on Geary near Mason and on Larkin and Golden Gate. Finally I got a steady gig at the Foster's at Polk and Sutter, first as a busboy, then graduating to short-order cook. It was there that I started meeting some people for the first time since I arrived.

The Foster's chain, which went defunct long ago, had some hot spots. The cafeteria at Polk and Sutter was one of them. Open 24 hours, it attracted a lot of the painters and writers who lived nearby. In fact, right overhead was the Hotel Bentley, immortalized by the poet John Wieners. Regulars included such artists as Wes Wilson, Ernie Nadalini, Byron Hunt, Robert LaVigne and his brother Harold, who was the first person I knew to take LSD (*long* before everyone else) and Rick Barton, who obsessively drew brilliant line drawings with a rapidograph pen in little black notebooks. True bohemians, they would come in late and hang out for hours, drawing and talking shit about everything   .

Among the suppertime regulars were a French woman who owned San Francisco's only French bookstore a half-block away on Polk and her pretty daughter who helped her mother in the store after school. The daughter was blond, stacked and seemed friendly. She didn't say much, but whenever I caught her eye she smiled. Not broadly, which might have meant, "This is my obligatory smile to everyone," but only slightly, as if against her will. I dug that.

Often, when it slowed down a little on the grill, I'd help out the busboy and bus a few tables. He didn't need any help on this particular night, but I noticed the French woman and her daughter at one of the tables winding up their meal. When the mother headed to the rest room. I grabbed a cart and made a bee-line.

"Hi," I famously said.

"Hi."

"My name's Mel."

"I'm Nicky."

"How was the meat loaf?"

"No surprises."

With that same subtle smile.

Over the next couple of days, she came in twice without her mother. The first time, she just ordered a cup of tea. I learned that she was a figure skater, that she dug Audrey Hepburn, and that she couldn't wait to graduate from Galileo High School in June. The second time, the very next day, she had a cup of tea again, and I found out that her mother was harsh and possessive. She sometimes beat her with an extension cord. When she was about to leave, I said, "I live at 920 Post, number six."

"Okay."

"I'm off tomorrow."

"Okay."

At 3:30 the next day my buzzer rang. She had just returned from Galileo and told her mother she needed to go to the library for a while.

"Is Nicky your real name?"

"No. Nicole."

"That's a nice name. Do you like it?"

"My mother wants me to stay a child, so I'll always be Nicky to her."

"I'm gonna call you Nicole, okay?"

"Okay."

Nicole was a virgin, 17 years old, almost 18. I was 26, almost 27. The disparity in age, more meaningless as one grows older, was considered a rather big deal at the time.

At first, Nicole told her mother one lie after another so she could steal away for a couple of hours of sex and conversation at my place. I'd make her tea, too, which she liked. I'd also make her snacks. Her favorite was a tuna fish sandwich with potato chips—*in* the sandwich.

After a couple of weeks of sneaking around, she defiantly admitted that she was seeing me. Her mother flipped, ordering Nicole never to see me again and demanding to know where I lived. When Nicole refused to say, her mother whacked her with the extension cord.

Nicole kept coming over anyway. Usually she would

take a roundabout route because she was convinced her mother's friend, a guy named Antoine, was following her. Turns out he was. I felt bad about being the cause of her troubles, and suggested we cool it until things settled down, but she wouldn't hear of it.

Even on her 18th birthday, her mother wouldn't let her go out if she wasn't with a friend of hers that her mother knew. Because she worked so much at the bookstore, Nicole didn't have many girlfriends, but one of them agreed to pick her up at the bookstore and, mother satisfied for the moment, walk the few blocks to a fish-and-chips joint on Geary where I was waiting for her.

The cloak-and-dagger stuff was kind of a turn-on for me but it was hell on Nicole. It came to a head one night when I was down on Market Street playing pool with my buddy Mike at the Palace Pool Room. The Palace was open all night and a scene of many a big game. Usually straight pool or nine-ball. When I was down-and-out, staying at the buck-a-night St. Regis on Fourth Street and couldn't find any work, Mike, a truly great pool player, who also stayed at the St. Regis (that's where I met him), would hustle a few bucks at the tables and we'd eat pretty good for 2-3 days.

Max, who managed the Palace, said I had a phone call from "some broad." Nicole had told me that the next time her mother hit her with the cord, she was leaving for good. That time came, and now she was asking me to come get her. She said her mother wouldn't let her leave the store, even though the store had closed. Her mother was in the bathroom, so when I didn't answer my phone at home, Nicole called the Palace because she knew I hung out there.

I jumped in my Nash Rambler parked on Taylor, took a left on Sutter and was on my way to Polk, but as I drove downhill approaching Larkin I saw an animated scene on the northwest corner that resembled an opera in progress. I saw Nicole and her mother who was pulling on her arm as Nicole fought to get out of her grip. A bunch of people stood around kibitzing and there were two cops on the scene. I pulled right over and got out. Her mother yelled, "There he is. Arrest him." Some of the crowd thought it was a good idea. I never said a word. The cops were the only ones not freaking out.

Nicole's mother, still holding onto Nicole's arm, was trying to make the case that since I had sex with her daughter I should be arrested. Finally, the drama was resolved forever when the cop shut everyone up and asked Nicole's mother, "How old is your daughter?" Nicole, who knew that her mother would never utter the word, screamed out, "Eighteen!" When her mother, with a reluctant nod of her head, indicated that it was so, the cop said, "Then she's legal and if she wants to run off with this guy, she can." The cops, with outstretched arms, created a path to allow Nicole and me to get in the car.

We pulled away slowly, the cast of 10-12 people in the rear-view mirror, all watching us. I made a full stop at Polk, turned on my directional signal and slowly turned left. Suddenly, finally, all of that was no longer in my rear view mirror or in Nicole's rear view mirror, and with a wonderful sense of triumph, we were cruising down Polk on our way to god knows where.

We found a place to live and stayed together for a couple of years. That was more than fifty years ago and we still stay in touch.

Jack's Great Idea

In 1967 Jack and I were sharing a house on Levant Street about half-way up the 17th Street hill where the planet streets are—Mars, Saturn, etc. The place was on a slope and had two levels and a terraced backyard with a nice view. Those were the days.

We had been sharing a flat on Waller, a short block off Haight Street but, after being crazy in a good way, the scene started getting crazy in a bad way. Meth started making inroads. You know the drill. Levant Street put us at a distance and we could lighten up a bit. We were still splitting tabs of acid but instead of walking on Haight and exposing our ass to everything, we could trip out in our terraced backyard.

On this particular Saturday morning I'm preparing to make coffee when the two girls, hella groggy, walk upstairs into the kitchen.

"We gotta get back home," Summer says. "Our parents are gonna kill us."

"Better have some coffee first," I say.

"I don't think so," Bambi says, looking over at Summer.

See, Summer and Bambi are seniors at Burlingame High School down the Peninsula. Jack and I met them earlier in the week when we did a poetry reading at their school. We both do reading gigs at local high schools for a program called Poetry-in-the-Schools, based on the SF State campus. Only a few hours a week but good money. Our readings were popular with the hipper students. We were writing about getting laid and getting high and the kids could relate. Jack occasionally gave out our address for students to send us their writings. Last night Summer and Bambi skipped the preliminaries and knocked on our door. The rest was a stoned-out blur. They were determined to get high with us and jump into the sack. The same sack, all four of us.

Summer brought her guitar and sang folk songs. She wrote some of the tunes. Very cool. She says, "Thanks for offering us coffee, Mel, but we really have to drive back home. We said our goodbyes to Jack and now..."

At which point they both give me a hug. Sweet.

They leave just as the kettle starts whistling. As soon as the front door closes I hear Jack coming up the stairs from our bedrooms.

"They gone?" he whispers.

"Gone."

"Is it eleven yet?"

"Almost."

"Manny said he'd drop off the kilo around eleven."

On cue our front doorbell rings. Usually Manny will hang out and get high with us but today he collects our fifty-five bucks and says he has to run to see his kid's school play. After he leaves, Jack picks up the package, wrapped in the usual shiny blue paper, and says, "What the hell is this?"

196

"What?"

"This key is light."

"What did you expect? A 2.2 pound kilo?"

"They're always a *little* light but not *this* light."

"Lemme see that."

I grab the package and bounce it around.

"It's normal light."

"Bullshit. It's *abnormally* light. Not even close."

"Even if it *is* abnormally light it's still a good deal."

He picks it up again and bounces it around.

"It's not even 1.5 pounds."

We go back and forth about it. Basically, I don't care.

"Does Fast Freddie still have our scale?" he asks.

"Yeah but he told me he broke it."

"How can you break a scale?"

I can think of several ways just off the top of my head but I concentrate on making the perfect pot of coffee instead.

"Damn," says Jack. He's really worked up about this. We're sitting at the table drinking our coffee when a light bulb goes on over his head.

"I've got a great idea."

And so it was that Jack and I get in our car—a '48

Buick Roadmaster we call Kate Smith that we bought together for fifty bucks each—and drive down to the Cala Market on Haight and Stanyan, a la the Furry Freak Brothers, to weigh the pot on a scale in the Cala Market produce section.

We pull into Cala's parking lot. Jack's got the pot in a Safeway shopping bag, a detail I hadn't considered. I start getting a bit nervous about this. If the cashier wants to look at what's in the Safeway bag we're kinda fucked. Before we get out of the car I say to him, "Have you figured out how we're gonna get out of there after we weigh the shit?"

"No."

Satisfied that we have no plan and thus don't have to worry about executing it, we walk over to the shopping carts. I grab one and we enter Cala Market. Jack is suddenly hungry so he pulls a fairly common Jack-ism. He grabs a package of cheese and opens it while we walk up and down aisles looking like we're shopping. When finally sated he drops the remains of the cheese package behind the boxed cereals. Finally we get to the produce section and throw our Safeway bag on the scale. Just as I thought, the scale says one and three-quarter pounds. About average for a kilo of Mexican. Jack is incredulous.

"Damn, that scale has gotta be off. "

"Uh-huh."

"That is no 1.75 pounds."

He walks over to the elderly produce clerk.

"Does that scale give correct weight?"

"It's pretty close," the guy says.

He looks over at me with his eyebrows raised.

"Did you hear that? *Pretty close*," Jack says triumphantly.

"Pretty close for bananas" I say. "We knew it wouldn't be a calibrated pot scale that weighs grams."

Jack's not satisfied but accepts it for the moment. Maybe by now he doesn't care, either. He wants one more bite of cheese before we leave so we walk back to the boxed cereals.

"We gotta buy a few things," I say. "You know, like we're customers."

"What do we need?"

"Everything. Chips, salsa, tuna, half and half, cookies, red vines..."

We cruise the aisles and pick up a few items. Most of the registers are open and busy. Jack notices this cashier at register #7 who looks kind of hip. In fact he looks like a raging pothead. Thick mustache, long hair in a ponytail. Glasses with wire frames. Cat could be John Lennon. We wait in line at this guy's register but, as we approach, his *replacement* arrives with a new cash drawer. Our guy signs out and by the time we get to the front of the line, our guy is gone and his replacement has taken over--an older woman who *doesn't* look like a raging pothead. Not even close.

Permit me to pause here to explain that Jack is not easily flummoxed by an awkward situation. Nor is he a guy who will ever admit defeat. This cat is resourceful. Last semester we drove out to State to register for classes. We arrive to find a mile-long line snaking out of the administration building across and around the entire campus. If you think Jack is gonna go to the back of that line then you just don't know him. He says follow me (and I do, man, I do) and goes inside the administration building right up to the front of the line and hands the woman behind the barred window a line of shit that is at once lengthy, complex and passionate. Professor Irwin Corey playing Hamlet. Don't ask. All I know is that we *both* got to register right then and there. Fifteen minutes later we were back in Kate Smith heading home.

Despite Jack's prowess at bullshit, I remain skeptical and am starting to get even more nervous than I was in the parking lot. As I take the half and half, the chips, the tuna, etc. out of the cart, I'm chatting up the cashier, trying to distract her from Jack who casually carries the Safeway bag under his arm, but she--The Replacement Cashier--zooms right to the heart of the matter and says, all business, "What's in the bag?"

Jack's response? "A bunch of pot."

"Really?" she says, and looks a bit taken aback. In fact, she doesn't know whether to shit or go blind.

"Really," Jack says, and then with a slow turn toward me, "An *abnormally* light kilo of Michoacan." Then back to her, "We needed to weigh it on your scale."

She is nonplussed but smiling.

Now the capper: "Would you care for a taste just because I like you?"

"I don't think my boss would approve."

"Are you sure? I could put some in a little altoids tin that I have on me."

Now she's blushing, and says, "No, thank you anyway."

"All right. At least I tried."

We pay for the groceries. In the parking lot I say, "Man, that was pretty slick. You surprised *me* more than her."

"Sometimes," Jack explains, "lying is the best way to go. Sometimes telling the truth is best. You just gotta know when to lie and when to tell the truth."

Words to live by. And words to write by.

The Day the Beatles Broke Up

In 1969, around mid-August, I got a call from a buddy of mine, Larry, who had a job teaching at Chico State. He and I and Jack used to run around together in the Haight Ashbury where he put out a literary magazine whose contributors included the three of us. He wanted to know if I would be interested in a teaching gig at the college. The instructor who was scheduled to teach two sections of creative writing for the next two semesters had to cancel suddenly because of some personal problem. I never knew what.

The irony here is that more than a decade earlier I had dropped out of Columbia in my junior year right after my father died. I tried it again at SF State in 1967 but dropped out for a second time. So I had no degree and no teaching experience, but I had a funky little book of poems, and when I say funky I mean *mimeographed and stapled*. Larry showed the department head that little book and, despite my lack of a degree or teaching experience, I got the gig. But in 1969 that's the way things were. Shit just happened.

The main logistical problem was the fact that I lived in Marin County and Chico was 175 miles away. I could hack that commute once a week but even twice a week would turn my world upside down. But Larry and the department head worked it out so that I could teach both classes at the same time! One three-hour class once a week—Thursdays at 4:00. And I was to start in two weeks.

I was living with my girlfriend Diane in a cabin under the redwoods in Woodacre. We had been together for two years and had an idyllic life there except that something was wrong with us and I didn't know what.

On my first Thursday as a teacher I woke up excited. I had already researched the best route. I'd go over the Richmond Bridge, then east on 80 and a little before Sacto I'd hook up with this connecting road to I-5 North and finally go off at Chico River Road east for the last 45 minutes. The day before I had gassed up my trusty Chevy wagon, checked the oil and made sure the tires had the right air pressure. Diane made me a couple of tempeh burger sandwiches while I put everything I'd need in a briefcase.

I got to Chico in about four hours. Equipped with an ID card and a parking permit I got in the mail just the day before, I wandered around a bit while making my way to the Humanities building where, I had been told, there was a bigger-than-normal size classroom that could comfortably hold my 38 students.

At 3:55 I walked into HUM 127 and was a bit surprised to see a packed house. This was a great group. We started bonding right away. When I told them I lived in Marin they were impressed. The Bay Area was a mecca for a lot of them. They'd often go to SF on weekends. And they knew Marin too, especially Fairfax. Actually, as I was to learn, Chico was also extremely hip. I told them Chico was kind of a Fairfax North, or Northeast. They dug that. They were curious about my situation. I explained that I was only in town once a week, that I drove 175 miles to be there. That really got the room humming.

After the intros we got down to business. I whipped out a poem of mine and just started reading. Then different students started jumping up and reading and taking comments, inspiring a lively back-and-forth.

At the mid-point break, an hour and a half in, a bunch of students approached me and said we shouldn't go on meeting at HUM 127. They lived in pretty big houses off campus and said it would be more comfortable to meet there. That sounded good. At the end of each class I'd announce the address of the next class.

Man, that was a kick in the head. Students would try to outdo each other with hospitality. There was always lots of food at the break, wine and, after the second week, pot. At first I told them to take it out in back during the break, figuring those who didn't smoke might not dig it. Turned out almost everyone smoked and the few who didn't were cool with it. So there we'd be, passing joints around the room and reading our poems. Like I said, this was 1969 and shit like that went down. Later, at any future era, someone would've complained, and I would've been fired slash arrested.

When that first class was in its final minute, several of the students asked me where I was staying in Chico. I was thinking of my buddy Larry or even a Motel 6 but they wouldn't hear of it. So I started staying Thursday nights at various students' houses. We'd have coffee in the morning and we'd get loaded and they'd roll me up a couple of bombers for the road.

Yeah those Chico kids spoiled me silly. But a funny thing happened in mid-February—my trusty Chevy wagon blew up. I saw smoke coming out of the hood one day driving down White's Hill. Car threw a rod. I couldn't afford another car and immediately realized my problem. I was going to have to hitchhike to Chico every week.

At first I thought of taking buses but when I looked into it I realized I'd have to take too many buses and connections would be difficult. Not to mention the expense. Also, social acceptance of hitchhiking was at its peak. So for the last three months of the school year I hitchhiked to Chico once a week and usually hitched back the next day, except for the times it rained or I just wasn't up to it and took a bus. If bus connections took forever to get back home it didn't matter. It only mattered getting to Chico by 4:00 on Thursday.

Now I would arrive at our class, sometimes just minutes before 4:00, with my backpack, a big smile and arms up triumphantly. I got a standing ovation every time. It blew their minds that I had hitchhiked 175 miles and actually got there on time. In fact, I was never late.

One day in mid-April Robbie, a student who put me up for the night, drove me out to the highway for my hitch home. I put my thumb out and the very first car pulled over, and that wasn't the first time or even second time that happened. Like I said, hitchhiking was fairly common. The hard part was getting a long ride, anything past Sacto. On this day I jumped into a maroon Volvo and was surprised to see a pretty young woman behind the wheel. She had dark hair, pale skin and a warm smile.

"Hi, how far are you going?" she asked.

"Marin County, a little north of San Francisco."

"I can take you as far as the East Bay."

Wow, that would be one of the longest rides I'd ever had.

"My name's Mel."

"I'm Molly."

She was a junior at Chico, about 20, 21, and wanted to be a teacher. She was through with classes for the rest of the week and was going home to Danville where she lived with her parents. When she found out I was a teacher at Chico and that I hitchhiked to school from Marin once a week she was a bit shocked.

We chatted easily, letting some silence happen occasionally. I had a couple of apples and I asked her if she wanted one. She did, so there we were eating apples and cruising along. After a while I felt comfortable enough to ask if she would like to smoke some pot. Looking straight ahead and smiling, she said, "Sounds like fun." I whipped out one of the bombers that Robbie had rolled for my trip. As always, the quality was first-rate. Most of these guys grew their

206

own stuff so it was always fresh and potent.

We stopped just once, to get gas. I gave her a ten and told her to fill it up. Gas cost about forty cents a gallon. We both used the rest rooms and I bought us a couple of bags of Have A Chips. When we hit the road again she decided to turn on the radio, and when she did we heard the news. The Beatles had officially broken up. John had already kind of dropped out but there had still been some hope, but now Paul said he was done and that meant it really was over. It hit both of us hard. Even though it was April, 1970 it was hard to accept that right then and there the '60s—"our decade"--were officially over. The dj said they were going to play Beatles tunes all day long into the night and into the next day with no commercial breaks.

As we listened to one tune after another—*Strawberry Fields Forever, I Saw Her Standing There, The Word, Hey Jude, Good Day Sunshine, We Can Work it Out, Let it Be*-- we talked about what the Beatles meant to us. I was profoundly influenced. I never thought that I would get a guitar and start writing songs but I did after listening to them for a while. Molly said the influence was probably even deeper for her because she wasn't even in high school when the Beatles hit the scene. They provided the background music for most of her life. We drove along in silence, working on our Have A Chips and deep in our thoughts.

When we went off 80 and started going southwest on 680 I checked my map. I saw that when she got a bit past Walnut Creek there was a junction where we'd have to part company. She'd have to go left and continue south on 680 to Danville and I'd have to start hitching west on 24 toward the Bay Bridge. In SF I'd get a bus home. Not bad. Ah but it was to be much better than that. Right after Walnut Creek she said, "How would you like to go into San Francisco and fool around for a while?" Not only would that be a direct ride into SF but "fooling around" with Molly sounded awfully good. "Yeah," I said. "I would love to do that." And so we did.

She told me her sister and her husband lived in a flat on Hayes around Divisidero. They were in Europe for a few weeks and Molly went into town once in a while to water their plants. She said we could just hang out there and relax. I couldn't think of a single flaw in her plan.

When we arrived she got right to watering the many plants. I wanted to help so she let me fill the containers but she did the watering herself because, she explained, some plants need more water than others. Hm. Yeah.

We sat on a couch and I asked if I could make a call. The phone was at the far end of the flat. I usually called home to give Diane a heads-up about when I'd be back. A couple of times when I called I thought someone else was there with her. Both times I heard movement in the background. It was faint and I might have been wrong but...

"Hello."

"Hi, it's me. How's it going?

"Good. Where are you?"

"I got a good ride but I'll probably be a while so just eat something yourself and I'll eat later."

Right at that moment I heard a muffled cough. Classic, right? Someone *was* there. I'd always thought so but never asked the question. Now I did.

"Is someone there?"

"Of course not."

Of course not? That's the wrong answer! The correct answer is either yes, so-and-so just dropped by, or it's no, which would be the standard lie. Of course not is the obvious lie, the panicky lie. I was face to face with the fact that when I left each week to go to Chico she was fucking some guy in our idyllic little cabin. Some guy that I probably knew.

"Okay," I said. "See ya."

After I hung up I stood there for a bit, just breathing in and out. I walked back to the living room and sat on the couch with Molly. The radio was on KMPX and that station was also playing Beatles all day and night with no commercials. Both of us just sat there. *She Loves You, Eleanor Rigby, Drive My Car, No Reply, Help, She's Leaving Home, Savoy Truffle, Day Tripper*, one after the other.

We turned and looked at each other for a while, a kind of getting-to-know-you look. Our faces got close and we kissed. Then we went into her sister's bedroom and made sweet, passionate, unforgettable love. She was so sensitive, so tender. Afterward we held each other for a long time as the day got dark. When I prepared to leave, she insisted on driving me to the bus stop at Fillmore and Lombard.

On the bus to Marin I thought about me and Diane splitting up. I didn't know exactly when. I wanted to finish the school year—there was about six more weeks to go-- and take it from there. It bothered me that our thing really wasn't the transcendent thing I thought it was. I felt disillusioned, a terrible feeling for a romantic idealist. I had to grow up. Everything ends. Even the Beatles.

The one thing that never did end was Molly. That's because we never saw each other again. I often thought of looking her up and she probably had the same thought but, for whatever reasons, we didn't, and I'm so glad we didn't because that meant there was no denouement, no tainting, no whiff of bullshit. We had a once-in-a-lifetime experience and, because of that, all these years later it remains a profound moment in my life, a pristine memory, uncorrupted.

Movie Night in the San Geronimo Valley

In 1975 I was still living in the Valley. I found peace there seven years earlier after San Francisco got too freaky. Marin was still okay but you could see the thing starting to come apart, just like I saw the Haight-Ashbury start to come apart a decade before. The rents had gone up, a lot of cool people were moving farther north and the garage-band scene was disappearing. More than that, a bourgy thing was taking over. Diane and I broke up after five years and we split the time with our three-year old daughter.

Just for the fun of it, my friend Augie and I decided to show movies at the Lagunitas Art Center. Classic double bills—the Marx Brothers, Bogart, '30s musicals, foreign films—which we got cheap in 16mm format. We charged two bucks and screened them on Fridays and Saturdays.

One Saturday night I was sitting by myself in the lobby waiting for *Grand Illusion* to end so I could lock up and go over White's Hill to Fairfax and dig the action there. In walks Pauline Rolfe who lived in Woodacre not too far from my mother-in-law cabin on Rock Ridge. She was active in the local art scene, and her house was a showplace near the top of the ridge where she lived with her husband, Andrew Rolfe, a real estate big shot in the county ("The Rolfe Group"). Pauline was about my age, late 30s, attractive, smart, offbeat. We weren't buddies or anything, but I got to know her a little since putting on the double bills. She'd catch most of the weekend movies, often by herself, sometimes with a girlfriend, and we'd get to chatting about this and that. She was too late for tonight's second feature and I figured she was meeting a friend here.

"Hey, Pauline."

"Hi, Mel. How's it going."

"Movie's almost over. Another half hour"

"I know. I've seen this one before, so..."

She walked around checking out the movie posters in the lobby. Then she came over and sat next to me, seeming a bit nervous. She looked at me and when I returned her look she looked away.

"What's up?"

"Oh, nothing." And then, "Just thought I'd come by and say hello."

Really?

Then she drops *this* on me: "Are you busy tonight after the movie gets out?"

"No. Nothing special."

 Pause. Now she was real nervous. She started to say something but decided against it. She shook her head and looked away.

"Everything all right?"

"Yes. Sure."

I just waited. Finally:

"How would you feel about coming by our place after you're through here and hanging out with me and Andrew?"

"Uh, that sounds okay."

"When I say 'hanging out' I mean something more. Do you know what I'm trying to say?"

"Mmm...I think so."

"Do you think you could be into that?"

"Uh, yeah."

"I feel so weird. It's so hard to say."

"That's okay. I'll be there."

She broke into a smile, said, "I'll see you then," and left.

Damn. A three-way with the president of the Valley Art Council and her big shot husband? I didn't even *know* Pauline that well and I met her husband just once.

The movie ended and a full house (about 30 Valley-ites) came out, including Augie, who had seen the movie for the second straight night. I dig movies but Augie is a true *cineaste*. I handed over the night's take, about eighty-five bucks, so he could deposit it in the morning.

"I'm heading over the hill to catch the music at the Sleeping Lady. Wanna come?"

"Nah," I say. "I'm just going home for now but if I change my mind I'll look for you at the Lady."

I didn't want to tell him what was up and dissipate the energy. Also, like Pauline, I was getting nervous myself. I also was thinking, yeah, they might just be trying to spice up their sex life, or they were planning to kill me and hide the body in their backyard like in a Clouzot flick.

I only lived about a mile down the hill from them so I decided to go home first and change into something appropriate for the occasion. Like clean underwear. I also brushed my teeth. In case they weren't planning to kill me and bury me in their backyard, I brought a couple of Thai sticks and zig-zags.

A little after 11:00 I drove up to their house. It was set back and had one of those ante-bellum semi-circular gravel driveways. I could see both of their cars in the garage. She had a Rover station wagon and he drove a yellow Porsche. I was driving an old big-ass Bonneville that I bought for a hundred bucks a few months back. It had a few holes in the muffler so I knew they heard me when I pulled up.

Pauline greeted me cheerily at the door. So cheerily that I thought maybe I was misreading the whole thing. Maybe the "something more" she wanted was for me to, I don't know, read a short story she was writing.

Her husband got up from the couch when I walked into the living room. He shook my hand with a firm grip. Like Pauline, he was good-looking and fit.

"Hi, Mel. Do you remember me."

"Hey, Andrew. Of course. Though it was a while ago. At someone's birthday party, if I remember."

"In fact, it was Pauline's birthday party at the Fairfax Country Club two years ago."

"Oh yeah. Great party."

Pauline came over with a bottle in each hand.

"I have a French red wine that's very expensive and a lovely chardonnay that's rather cheap but very good. And while you're thinking about that, I also have gin, vodka and tequila. Andrew makes a lovely martini."

"Let's start with the expensive wine."

We sat on their wrap-around leather couch. The wine was good and the banter was lively. I didn't know what to think.

"How is your daughter?" Pauline asked.

"Oh, great."

"She's sooo cute."

"Yeah. It's not my weekend, so I'm free as a bird. Who is the little girl in that photo on the mantel?"

"Oh, that's my niece. My sister's daughter. She's ten now. They live in San Diego. I drive down there as much as I can."

Andrew was in his mid-40s and Pauline was pushing 40 so I figured if they hadn't had kids yet, they weren't going to.

I never thought of myself as a sex object. For good reason. But I figured Pauline felt safe with me because I had a daughter who lived with me half the time and was thus a responsible cat who wouldn't be blabbing about this all over the valley.

"I brought some killer pot if you're interested."

"Pot makes me sleepy," Andrew said. "But I've got some excellent cocaine. Do you indulge?"

Andrew had the stuff on him and he whipped it out and cut three fat lines right on the glass-top coffee table. Soon the three of us were quite ripped. We were getting along very nicely but I was still confused. That is until Pauline got up and sat between us on the couch. She held my hand then reached over to hold Andrew's hand. I guess this is it.

She leaned back, tilting her head toward me. She moistened her lips just before we kissed lightly. I looked over at Andrew and he was smiling.

Then Pauline, this woman that I hardly knew, threw

one leg over me and got on top of me, kissing me and grinding on my lap. If she was trying to give me a raging hard-on, it worked. All this seemed to fascinate Andrew. He looked on approvingly. I wondered if this was their first time or if they had made this scene before. Maybe often.

Pauline stood up and said, "Let's go into the bedroom."

She took my hand and Andrew's hand and walked us into their inner sanctum, featuring a huge four-poster bed, dim lights and sandalwood incense. I figured it was time to stop waiting for her cues and get proactive. Before we got to the bed I spun her around, put my free hand up her dress and started playing with her pussy outside of her pink panties. This aroused all three of us. We tore off our clothes and jumped onto the silk sheets. Pauline was on fire, breathing heavy, the whole bit. I was working her over when Andrew, who had been on her other side, jumped over both of us and now I was in the middle. Right away Andrew grabbed my erect penis.

"Hey man, knock that shit off. Ain't happening, okay?"

He immediately backed away and looked hurt. So that's where this whole thing is at. Andrew is gay or bi, and they don't have much sex or *any* sex anymore. Pauline must've thought maybe I'd go for the bi thing or, if not, at least Andrew might get turned on to her if he saw me fucking her. Despite, or because of, this tangled web, I got even hotter for Pauline. She obviously needs a good fuck and if it turns Andrew on to her, that's a twofer. As I started pounding away at Pauline Andrew was on his knees right next to us beating off, having a good old time. Sometimes she'd reach out for his dick and stroke it.

After a while Pauline started to come, over and over. It was a beautiful sight. I pulled out of her and rolled over to rest a bit. She reached over to Andrew with both arms and tried to pull him toward her but he kept his distance, checking me out and beating off. The disappointed look on her face got me out of the mood real fast. When she turned to me again I had gotten soft. She sucked my dick until it got hard again and we resumed our fuckfest. After a while she told me I could cum inside her and when I saw that she wanted me to, I did. Kablooey. I rolled off of her on her right side. Andrew then came all over her left arm which she wiped off with a nearby towel. The three of us were drained and in a few minutes we all fell asleep.

I woke up a couple of hours later. It was still dark out but you could feel the morning light coming on. I got out of bed quietly and put my clothes on. As I walked toward the bedroom door I noticed a framed photo on her Victorian desk. It was of her ten-year old niece. I looked back at them, one last look. They were both fast asleep. He was snoring.

At first I rolled the Bonneville slowly down the slight incline of the semi-circular driveway, not wanting to wake them up. Then I decided, fuck it. I revved the engine and gunned it out of there, the muffler booming and my tires grinding on the gravel. I headed back to my perfect little mother-in-law cabin on Rock Ridge, thinking I had to get the hell out of the valley, out of Marin, back to San Francisco.

Mel and Dee and the Great Unknown

I think it was 1991 when I first met Dee at a party one Saturday night on Webster Street in the Fillmore. The crowd was mostly musicians and others who were into the music. Benny, a bass player I had jammed with a couple of times, told me he held sessions like this at his flat. He called me out of the blue and asked me to come over and sing a few tunes.

It didn't hit me until I walked in the door that I didn't know a soul except Benny and I didn't even recognize him at first because of a beard he had grown. Usually, a singer doesn't have the luxury of playing with the same musicians—they're either gigging or rehearsing with various bands or doing the family thing—so I seek out venues like this to get my work in. A singer without a band is a pathetic figure, if you want to know.

I got a glass of red wine and leaned against a wall to listen. Dee stood behind this little keyboard on a stand and sang with bass, drums and a couple of horns. She was working on *But Beautiful*, eyes closed most of the time a la Chris Connor.

> *Love is funny or it's sad,*
> *or it's quiet or it's mad.*
> *It's a good thing or it's bad,*
> *But Beautiful...*

She sang it sweet and straight and I loved it. Then they did a run-for-cover *Rhythm-a-ning* and she killed it, slapping and pecking at that little keyboard, dominating it. I was on the ropes by the time she got into *Say It Isn't So*.

> *...Tell me everything is still okay.*
> *That's all I want to know.*
> *And what they're saying—*
> *Say It Isn't So.*

On "okay" she showed her vulnerability. I was crazy about her before the tune ended. I finished my glass of wine and was still high on the pinner I smoked on the way over. I was reading the crowd and wondering which one of the tunes I brought I would sing first. I decided to shock the world and start with a ballad. When there was a pause for a new drummer, Benny gave me the high sign to come on up.

Dee had become that one person I always need to sing for. That person understands everything I'm doing, every nuance and every departure. I was lucky tonight. It was Dee and she was even playing behind me.

I put my first chart, *Blame It on My Youth*, on her music stand and gave a copy to the bass player. She bobbed her head up and down and sat down at the upright. I counted out a slow tempo.

> *If I expected love when first we kissed,*
> *Blame It on My Youth.*
> *If only just for you I did exist,*
> *Blame It on My Youth...*

I was concentrating on the spaces between the words.

> *If you were on my mind both night and day,*
> *Blame It on My Youth.*

> *If I forgot to eat or sleep or pray*
> *Blame It on My Youth.*

I understood the "pray" part for the first time. Forgot to pray that the affair would never end, of course.

> *If I cried a little bit*
> *when first I learned the truth,*
> *don't blame it on my heart,*
> *Blame It on My Youth.*

On "a little bit" I showed my own vulnerability, and I even thought Dee picked up on it by what she played. The applause seemed sincere. I only brought a few tunes with me because Benny told me that three or four other singers were going to be there and I noticed them—all females—leaning against the same wall I had leaned against. I whipped out *Tangerine* and passed it to Dee who seemed to like that one, too. That was all I needed. I counted out a tempo that kicked without rushing it.

> *...Yes, she's got them all on the run,*
> *but her heart belongs to just one.*
> *Her heart belongs to Tangerine.*

I realized as I sang those lines that Dee *was* Tangerine. While the alto was blowing a couple of choruses, my mind raced ahead. She already had me on the run and we hadn't even met. The people seemed to like that one, too. I thought of the singers waiting to go on and I went with my favorite rule of thumb: better too little than too much. I said I'd sing one more and went for broke with *Speak Low*.

Speak Low when you speak love.
Our summer day withers away
too soon, too soon.

The bass and drums were doing a subdued bolero thing, and the horns—alto and trombone—blew long tones behind me, a net I could fall into if I needed it. But that's the thing: to find where the edge is, to get on it and stay there, and if you fall off because you lose control, even better.

Speak Low, darling, Speak Low.
Love is a spark lost in the dark
too soon, too soon.

Dee's piano made commentaries, filling spaces with both conventional harmonies and dissonance, probing, wanting more. I gave her more. Swinging tempo on the bridge.

Time is so old
and love so brief.
Love is pure gold
and time a thief.

Now Dee's accents played off mine. And whenever I put out a feeling, she underlined it.

We're late, darling, we're late.
The curtain descends, everything ends
too soon, too soon.
I wait, darling, I wait.
Will you Speak Low to me ,
speak love to me
and soon.

We never did talk that night. Later, before I left, Benny mentioned that Dee was the house pianist at a bar called Mildred's at Polk and Post and that musicians came by to jam on Tuesday nights. The only rule was—bring your own charts. He looked at me as if to say, do it.

Three days later, the very next Tuesday, I did. At about 11:30 I found a parking spot on Van Ness and as I walked the couple of blocks down Post I gave myself my A speech: Remember, you're here for the music. Whatever else happens, cool. And if nothing happens, also cool. Go with what got you here.

When I walked in I could hear Dee without seeing her. Mildred's is an L-shaped room and Dee was around the corner at the baby grand singing *For All We Know*. I flipped. That was one of the tunes I brought with me. I stopped without entering farther. I didn't want to make eye contact with her until she finished. I sidled over behind the cigarette machine and listened.

> *...For All We Know, this may only be a dream.*
> *We come and go just like ripples on a stream.*
> *So love me tonight, tomorrow was made for some,*
> *tomorrow may never come, For All We Know.*

The applause was scattered, if that, despite the fairly packed house, partly because she was tucked in that corner, partly because the patrons were smashed and hustling each other, and partly because Dee's low-key approach didn't make an appeal to the audience. She was above it all. I turned the corner and finally saw her. She was wearing a plain black dress that killed. When I spoke to her it was for the first time.

"Hi, Dee."

"Hi."

"Mel."

"Yeah. I hope you're not just here to drink."

"I brought a couple of things."

She was noodling around with some chords and I backed off a little so she could stretch out. As I pondered my next move, she said, without looking up, "What've you got?"

I threw a few charts on the piano and said, "Let's air out some blues in F. You know *Bongo Beep*?"

She smiled, still looking down at the keyboard, and answered the question by playing the tune's opening few bars and then stopped playing abruptly.

I took the mike off the stand, looked Dee straight in the eye, serious as a heart attack, and counted out a swinging tempo. I had written a lyric to one of Bird's tunes and after the head I scatted a bunch of choruses as Dee let out some whoops. She was playing some nice stuff behind me, walking the bass for a nice stretch. It's fun singing along with nothing but a walking bass line. I was in heaven.

The applause went from scattered to appreciative. Dee and I looked at each other and smiled. I wanted to slow it way down. I didn't want it to end.

> *Ev'rytime We Say Goodbye I die a little.*
> *Ev'rytime We Say Goodbye I wonder why a little...*

I was looking at Dee, singing to her from the other side of the baby grand.

> *When you're near there's such an air*
> *of spring about it.*
> *I can hear a lark somewhere*
> *begin to sing about it...*

I was right where I wanted to be. Just me, Dee and the song.

> *There's no love song finer,*
> *but how strange the change*
> *from major to minor*
> *Ev'rytime We Say Goodbye.*

For the first time the sad ending hit me.

We did a high vibe *Have You Met Miss Jones.* Miss Jones, like Dee, was offbeat and compelling, and the guy in the tune is skeptical and detached—at first. He quickly becomes a believer in the bridge. The crowd dug it. I decided to end it there. I said thanks with a little wave, walked over by the piano bench and slid the mike back on the stand. Dee gave me big eyes.

"You slayed 'em."

"You made it easy."

"It was fun."

Benny said *do* it.

"Are you through at two or what?"

"One-thirty."

"Let's do something."

She started working over some chords, smiling at the keyboard, and finally said, "What's your plan?"

"No plan."

I was trying to keep it simple. I figured she had heard it all. She suddenly looked up at me.

"Okay."

I waited for her at the bar where I couldn't see her but I could hear. The uptempo stuff had a bright west coast feel. She could get dark on the ballads, though. I dug that. I wondered if she was married with two kids or what the hell the deal was. Dee was ready right at 1:30. She had a car too and told me to follow her to her apartment on Montgomery and Green in North Beach.

We were drinking a bottle of this Mouton-Cadet that she said she got cheap at Coit Liquors right down the hill. We got comfy and talked mostly about music. She didn't have a husband and two kids. She had been married, though, to a musician from Vegas where they lived and worked. She played in a scantily-clad all-girl band and made good money.

Dee had a gorgeous piano, a shiny white spinet that was placed right in the middle of her living room. There was nothing else in the room except a couch and a coffee table where she said she always ate. We were sitting on that couch when she said, "Are you waiting for the right moment to make your move?"

"Yeah."

We chuckled a little, then she leaned toward me. I kissed her softly. She touched my face and I stroked her cheek.

"How old are you?" she said.

"Fifty-six."

"Are you disappointed in me for asking?"

"Yeah."

"Do you want to know how old I am?"

"No."

"I'm thirty-six...let's do a tune."

We went over to the piano. She sat down and said, "Pick your poison."

"How about *My Foolish Heart.* Can you play it in Bb?"

"Of course. I can play in any key."

"I would get on the floor and kiss your feet if we weren't sitting on a piano bench. Too awkward for a first date."

She knew I was only half-kidding. Singers desperately need musicians who can transpose--without losing anything.

The night is like a lovely tune.
Beware, My Foolish Heart...

> There's a line between love and fascination
> that's hard to see on an evening such as this,
> for they both have the very sensation
> when you're lost in the magic of a kiss...

> ...For this time it isn't fascination
> or a dream that will fade and fall apart.
> It's love. This time it's love, My Foolish Heart.

Now she wanted me to play. I'm a low-echelon hacker compared to Dee but I told her I would if she sang. She flipped through one of her fake books and then put it on the piano. *All or Nothing at All.* I was afraid of this.

> All or Nothing at All.
> Half a love never appealed to me.
> If your heart never could yield to me
> then I'd rather have nothing at all...

> And if I fell under the spell of your call
> I would be lost in the undertow.
> So you see I've got to say no, no,
> All or Nothing at All.

We both stood up at the same time, kicked back the piano bench and kissed. Then she took my hand and led me into her bedroom. Still holding hands, we dove on the bed and held each other close. When the breathing started to pick up, she said, "Wait a minute."

Before we went any further she wanted me to sing something to her right there with the lights off, "with all your heart." The first song that popped in my head was *Dancing in the Dark* because it reminded me of *For All We Know*, a song I wanted to sing earlier about seizing the moment and living in the now.

> *Dancing in the Dark, 'til the tune ends*
> *we're Dancing in the Dark, and it soon ends.*
> *We're waltzing in the wonder of why we're here.*
> *Time hurries by, we're here and gone.*
>
> *Looking for the light of a new love*
> *to brighten up the night. I have you love*
> *and we can face the music together*
> *Dancing in the Dark...*

Then I made her sing to me. She thought for a while, then brought her mouth up to my ear.

> *Alone Together, beyond the crowd,*
> *above the world, we're not too proud*
> *to cling together—*
> *we're strong as long as we're together...*
>
> *Our love is as deep as the sea.*
> *Our love is as deep as a love can be.*
> *And we can weather the great unknown*
> *if we're Alone Together.*

I made a snap decision that I knew I'd have trouble living with.

"I gotta go."

She thought I meant to the bathroom.

"This is hard to explain," I said as I rolled away. "I just about understand it myself."

She stared at me as I pulled on my pants and tucked my shirt in. I put my shoes back on and was completely dressed when she said to me in a low voice, "Why?"

"Because I don't want to mess up what we've got musically."

She wrinkled her brow. She didn't understand.

"I went too far and I created an awkward situation. I apologize for that."

"Mel..." she said in disbelief.

"Better too little than too much."

She stared at me.

I said, "You know how things can go sour and then you lose everything."

She sat up in bed, still staring, and said, "Maybe you're right, maybe not. Let it happen."

We stayed frozen for a few moments. She wanted more.

"All right, here's the deal. I'm married--with two kids. I'm truly sorry."

She flopped back down, looking at the ceiling.

"I thought I could keep it strictly music but I was wrong, very wrong."

"All right, then, just go."

Now she was pissed.

"I'm going to want to play with you soon."

"I don't know."

"I just want to concentrate on the music."

Long pause, then "Big maybe."

"That's good enough for me."

I knelt down next to her and tried to kiss her but she turned her head. I caressed her cheek with the back of my hand and smoothed out her hair.

"I really admire you," I said.

She was done talking. I straightened up and let myself out.

I drove out Geary to the Avenues where I live, feeling like shit and working on the roach in the ashtray. I turned on KJAZ but wasn't listening. I turned it off and sang.

> *Love is tearful or it's gay,*
> *it's a problem or it's play,*
> *it's a heartache either way,*
> *But Beautiful.*

When I got back to the apartment it was a little after 4:00. My roommate was already up, finishing his morning coffee. He works at the airport and has weird hours. He wanted to chitchat but I went straight to my room and tried to sleep. It'll take a couple of days but she'll get over it, whereas an old affair would've ended everything. And it's a bitch trying to find a piano player who can *transpose*.

Epilogue: Gentlemen Songsters

This happened in Oban, Scotland. Me, 81, walking along the waterfront with Pamela, digging the nautical scene. Suddenly, as is my wont, I latch on to a song. *The Wiffenpoof Song*. When I get into a song, sometimes for days, I always wonder: Why *that* song? I usually know right away. This time I didn't. Then I did.

> *"From the tables down at Mory's, to the place where Louie dwells, to the dear old Temple Bar we know so well."*

Back in the, oh, mid-1950s we Milford guys knew all about the Temple Bar in New Haven (full name: Mory's Temple Bar, Louie ran the place). It was just eight or nine miles down the road. We'd go into New Haven a lot to eat pizza (where the whole pizza thing started in the U.S.), to go to some bars that would let us drink even though we were all under age, to check out the Yale Art Gallery (we all dug this big Tchelitchev painting called Hide and Seek), to go to the Lincoln Theater, the only place you could watch the great foreign flicks, and we'd go to the Yale Bowl on Saturday afternoons in September, October and November, the damp red and yellow and orange leaves under our feet as we walked to the Bowl. Yale had a black player, a running back named Levi Jackson. Number 40.

> *"...sang the Wiffenpoofs assembled with their glasses raised on high and the magic of their singing cast its spell."*

Yeah that would be us, me and Stewie and Danny and Tony and Johnny, others sometimes but only sometimes. We were the hardcores. We lived to sing— and we assembled on one of the corners in downtown Milford, at Paul's hamburger stand out on Boston Post Road, wherever, but mostly on the beach during the warm months--Bayview Beach, Pond Point, Gulf Beach. Stewie used to say, "You drive, you're too drunk to sing." Our glasses raised on high were filled with beer, occasionally hard stuff. Scotch mostly. We hadn't discovered pot yet. In fact I was the only one of us who did discover it a few years later and that was the end of my booze career. We would usually try to get some girls to go down to the beach with us. We often did find girls but most of them didn't join in on the singing, especially the folk stuff. They didn't know the tunes. Yeah we were interested in sex, very interested, but none of us had ever had any. We were about 16, 17 and hadn't even had girlfriends. A primal moment came one early summer evening when we were cruising around near the Ship Ahoy, our go-to hotdog stand on the main drag at the beach, and saw these girls who had gone to the beach with us before. We said hey jump in and let's go to Bayview and they shot back, "What do you want to do, go to the beach and *sing*?" said with extreme sarcasm and a touch of contempt. Well, yeah, that kind of *was* what we were thinking but, uh…Those girls pinned us. They were calling us out as pathetic nerds. We laughed it off and it became a private joke for a long time but it cut deeply. No, we might have said to the girls, we're not fags but, all in all, especially considering the era, we'd rather sing. Yeah we bonded by singing, and it was a strong bond.

"Yes the magic of their singing of the songs we know
so well, Shall I Wasting and Mavourneen and the rest..."
The songs *we* knew so well were *Trying* by Jimmy Sacca and the Hilltoppers, *You're Mine* by Shirley Gunner and the Queens (on the Duotone label), *Sh-Boom, The Tennessee Waltz, You Win Again, Goodnight Irene, Earth Angel, Ricochet Romance*, cowboy songs, calypso songs, a lot of folk stuff, *The Sloop John B, Across the Wide Missouri, Hard Trav'lin'*. Stewie played the ukulele and knew all kinds of obscure stuff--*Fox went out on a chilly night/prayed to the moon to give him light/many a mile to go that night/before he reached the town-o, town-o, town-o/many a mile to go that night before he reached the town.* Stewie was the only guy who played an instrument, except Johnny who played the guitar but rarely had it with him. During the mid-'50s playing an instrument was a bit unusual. Guys who played an instrument were training to be professionals. Period. Tony and I were the only ones into jazz, and we sang a lot together. With the songfests at the beach I was the harmony guy. I did simple step harmonies to fill out the sound but doing standards with Tony I'd get much further out and used a lot of off-beat and dissonant harmonies. It was pretty exciting, just creating as you went along.

"We will serenade our Louie while life and voice shall last,
then we'll pass and be forgotten with the rest."

233

All of us were pretty much geniuses but Johnny was the biggest genius of all. He, who grew up in poverty and dropped out of high school *in his freshman year*, would walk into a bar with his guitar, spontaneously, boom, there he was, and just start playing minor chords, like E minor to A minor, back and forth, while reciting 20 to 30 verses of the Rubaiyat. From memory, you understand. It was quite moving. He turned me on to Charles Dickens. By age 17 he had read all of Dickens' novels. *All of them.* He turned me on to John McCormack, the Irish tenor, singing all these great Irish songs. He turned me on to Buddy Holly whom I, a jazz snob, hadn't paid close attention to. Danny was no slouch in the genius department. He loved Beethoven's Moonlight Sonata, the first movement, so he just learned the whole thing. By ear. He never pursued piano playing after that. Even just for fun. Playing that piece was simply something he wanted to do and he did it. We would also air-conduct various pieces of classical music. Beethoven's Fifth was a favorite. Also Tchaikovsky, especially the violin concerto. Tony and John were both into opera and both took bel canto lessons in New Haven. Tony sang arias from various operas. He loved Puccini. Tony could sing the male and female roles at the end of Act One of *La Boheme.* Break your heart.

> *"We're poor little lambs who have lost our way,*
> *baa baa baa..."*

The Wiffenpoof Song is based on a poem by Rudyard Kipling called Gentlemen Rankers. Rankers were common soldiers from the poor classes but *gentlemen* rankers were from the wealthy upper classes, guys who were different, who didn't want to manage dad's chain of factories, who were gay perhaps, rebels, dreamers, who, for one reason or other, would bring embarrassment to the family or family name, who were sent off to Burma and Khartoum to fight in colonial wars. I met gentlemen rankers when I spent my senior year at a prestigious prep school that happened to be in Milford, the Milford School. They were rich kids from Long Island, Manhattan, Jersey, not to mention Venezuela, Colombia, the Philippines, rich kids whose parents didn't want them around so they were sent off, not to war zones but to boarding schools. I was a townie, one of a handful of Milford kids who went there, mostly on scholarships. We all played on the basketball team. During lunch we wore white jackets, took trays of food from the dumbwaiter in the middle of the lunch room and served the students, rankers all.

    "We're little black sheep who have gone astray,
      baa baa baa..."
Yeah that was us exactly. Just having fun and daring anyone to stop us. Down to the beach or on any street corner. We passionately believed that going to college was selling out, having a career was selling out, *getting a job* was selling out. And selling out was the worst thing you could do. The most heinous crime. Worse than armed robbery. Much worse.

    "Gentlemen songsters off on a spree..."
Yes, that was us. Off on a spree, man. Going nowhere and wasn't it great.

"...doomed from here to eternity..."
Yes, yes, doomed. Stewie was the only one of us to go to college and graduate. The rest of us tried it for a while but dropped out. Stewie was different. He never got a grade lower than an A in high school (a tough private school) or in college. I'm talkin' Yale. Valedictorian. Summa Cum Laude. Every year. Forget it. He was equally versed in science and literature, and you don't see *that* very often. He wanted to be a doctor so, after a rigorous pre-med undergraduate curriculum which he killed, he applied to Yale Medical School and a few others. He was quickly rejected by all of them. Yeah, a guy with probably the best academic record of all time, rejected by every one of them. See, there was a quota at the time. Only a few Jews were accepted at elite med schools. He wound up getting a teaching certificate at some blue collar school, Southern Connecticut I think it was, and taught English at a vocational high school in Newtown for many years. Stewie died of a heart attack at age 53.

"Lord have mercy on such as we! Baa, baa, baa."
No mercy for Stewie. The rest of us are still text-book misfits. Great guys all but misfits. Non-joiners who never fit into anything. But, except for Stewie, we did survive, didn't we? Me, Dan, Tony, Johnny. We're all in our 80s now. We made it. Shocker of shockers. Goes to show, even misfits survive.

Heck of a story. That's what I'm thinking as I walk along the Oban waterfront, deep in this memory. I started singing as I strolled along. Pam is used to me breaking into song, "To the tables down at..." but I couldn't get to "Mory's." My throat got too tight and nothing came out. When I was born it was the beginning of the end. I understand that now. But it ain't the end yet. Maybe there's still time.

www.ingramcontent.com/pod-product-compliance
Lightning Source LLC
Chambersburg PA
CBHW050732180626
46814CB00002B/723